The Art of Losing

A Novel

JANET HUBBS

authorHOUSE®

AuthorHouse™
1663 Liberty Drive
Bloomington, IN 47403
www.authorhouse.com
Phone: 1 (800) 839-8640

This is a work of fiction. Any resemblance to persons or situations in real life or time is purely coincidental.

Published by AuthorHouse 11/09/2015

ISBN: 978-1-5049-6042-7 (sc)
ISBN: 978-1-5049-6041-0 (e)

Print information available on the last page.

One Art
The art of losing isn't hard to master;
so many things seem filled with the intent
to be lost that their loss is no disaster.

Elizabeth Bishop, 1976

Part One:
Courtship and Marriage

"...till death do us part."

CHAPTER 1

I went to my ex-husband's funeral. I didn't go because I'm a good sport (defined by me as doing something I don't want to do that somebody else wants me to do). I'm not a good sport. I also didn't go because I still sort of loved him (although I did; everyone still sort of loved him). I went because they needed people to sit in the front row and be his family, so why not my daughter and me? I was no longer his wife and my daughter was never his daughter, but once upon a time the three of us all lived under the same roof, and so I guess we qualified as family almost as well as his two real daughters and two granddaughters who rarely saw him but were his only active blood relatives, not counting a son whom no one could find and a brother whom no one wanted to find.

Jimmy was eighty-one when he died from cancer, living in Florida, picking up women in bars to sleep with him (I'm not too sure conventional sex was involved by that time) and then to drive him to the hospital in the morning for his chemo treatments. I understand he missed several treatments which may or may not have contributed to his death but obviously fed his libido. He wouldn't have cared either way, actually. I recall when we were getting divorced; he went to a local pub quite regularly to eat and drink and sat at the bar handing out his business card to every woman in the place. He'd say, I'm getting divorced; give me a call. At the time, I was forty-five and he was sixty. I didn't plan on ever getting married again, and I didn't, but he didn't rule it out. In fact, Jimmy ruled nothing out during his entire life. Getting to his chemo on time would never really be a priority since his life's mantra was: I'm never going to die, and he meant that quite literally.

He was diagnosed as bi-polar after we separated, shortly before we divorced, but were I ever asked for an opinion (which I wasn't), I'd have said he was "unipolar," no such word but there ought to be, meaning: all manic. I don't ever remember really seeing him as depressive or depressed. God knows he could get angry as hell, which was probably his shield, his defense against depression, but he was never really down in the mouth. In fact, when I was married to him, although I knew he was an eccentric person in some very peculiar way, perhaps even neurotic, I never knew that he had a diagnosable mental illness. I certainly spent enough time reading psychobabble and trying to figure him out, but bi-polar never entered my mind. No "bi" there. One night when we were having a drink at the bar of his golf club before dinner, he asked his friend John if John thought he, Jimmy, might be going through male menopause. John told him no because you had to finish puberty before you could go through menopause. I think the chances are good, quite seriously, that Jimmy did not ever quite finish puberty, at least psychologically. I think he was having too much fun as a wayward teen to ever quite give it up completely. I truly spent many hours when we were married trying to decide whether Jimmy was a happy boy or a tortured soul. As it turned out, he was both.

There was always this myth that when Jimmy died there would be twenty or more hysterical ex-wives and lovers weeping at the casket, shoving each other out of the way. In fact, I was the only ex-wife there. The first wife by this time had Alzheimer's and was institutionalized. The second wife was in the wind, having given Jimmy the slip for a younger and presumably richer man: younger, yes; but richer, as it turned out, not so much. For the few years before she married her third husband, wife two (the one before me) had driven around in a Mercedes convertible with a license plate that read 2-X, implying that Jimmy had paid for the car (I don't think he did). There had never been a fourth wife for Jimmy as everyone, including me, had supposed there would be. And it was not ever about being rich, because Jimmy was not rich. He had been sort of rich, on and off, had owned a seat on the NY Stock Exchange when they weren't as expensive as they got, had owned a kind of showy house for a while that looked a little like old money and a little like a faux French Chateau, but Jimmy could never really hang on to anything for any significant length of time—not the wives, not the house, and certainly not the money, although he always found a way to have enough or to look like he had more.

He had wonderful humor, a great deal of charm, good clothes, good taste, a very good golf game, superior bridge and backgammon skills, and a lot of either rich or famous (or both) friends whom he guarded jealously and hung onto, lightly but tenaciously, over the years. He once told me that rich people needed people to visit them—to come for dinner, stay for the weekend, play golf with them, fly down to their Caribbean villas—and that he was that person. He used to call himself America's Guest and specialized in guest-hood, a good specialty for a man willing to let anything and everything go, so long as he could put on his J. Press or Brooks Brothers' suits (this was pre-Armani), Gucci loafers, his Burberry raincoat—and take off for points rich. Doing this, he was a happy man. And he was right, people always need guests, especially charming, good-looking slender men who are silver-haired, six feet four inches tall with wit and an assured physical grace. He did brighten up the scene.

He also loved re-naming people. He would apply different nicknames to many of the cast of characters that populated his life, but no nickname ever stuck more than his own: Captain Jimmy, like a children's cereal or a TV cartoon hero. Just about everyone who knew him called him that, at least part of the time, except me. You're not my captain, I once told him.

Obviously, he was not easy to be married to, but when I agreed to try it, I wasn't looking for easy. His first wife is supposed to have said this to his second wife: He's not a great husband, but you'll never be bored. Jimmy delighted in telling me this and it may actually have been original with him rather than his first wife; but no matter who originated the observation, it was only partially true. He really wasn't a totally horrible husband. It was more like having a cross between a teenager to raise, not boring, and some 1950s version of father-knows-best, stultifying and unimaginative, quite predictable and tedious. Oddly, the reason I divorced him in the end was more the latter rather than the former. The amusing teenager I could handle most of the time, but not the boring, stereotypical, mid-century stern husband, beset by the rules that the image conferred on me, on the marriage, and these rules all blurred by the personality disorder into something beyond bizarre. Contrary to the myth, he could really be very dull on the home front, when he wasn't being willful, often fixated on routine, with obsessive-compulsive arrangements of household items, ritual practices like taking the wife out to dinner on (*every*) Saturday night, or having hamburgers *every* Sunday night after whatever seasonal sport was on TV (but, he'd say, I *like* hamburgers). It was as if he had regressed to some distorted memory of either his own father or the iconic TV sit-com father and it was ghastly and eventually depressing for me, his obsessions and his special brand of lunacy that emerged amidst all the boredom.

He naturally told everyone he was divorcing me, which was fine. Who cared? By that time, I was just trying to get out alive; because, with my increasing rejection of him and his hum-drum routines, came the schizoid break that was no longer funny or eccentric or not-boring or even boring. It was something else entirely.

But it was a nice funeral. His daughters did a very good job organizing it and getting his remains from Florida to New Jersey and arranging for the church. Jimmy would have liked it. It was held in a very old Episcopal church in the very upscale town of Rumson, New Jersey, a town where Jimmy had once lived in his impressive Chateau for a while with his first wife and three children. They lived there as a family, although one could not exactly call it a normal family, when heading it was a father who would pick up women at parties where he'd leave his wife in the care of friends and then fly off to Lyford Cay or Bermuda with his pickups. This is just one of the many things that made Jimmy perpetually scandalous, in Rumson and on Wall Street, which is perhaps why he did it, in addition to all that fun. It was only one of many things recalled by the mourners at his funeral as we all stood on the sidewalk outside the lovely old fieldstone church before the service, talking about wonderfully outrageous Jimmy. It was a gorgeous spring day, sunny, cool-warm, tree leaves that were that kind of Granny Apple green color they get in spring, partially transparent and filled with light.

I hadn't seen most of the people who were there at the funeral service for a long time, some not since my divorce. They all looked old. Jimmy's friends were Jimmy's friends—always nice to me, always waiting for Jimmy to dump me, always getting set for the new wife or girlfriend they'd come to believe there would always be. It took a certain wry tolerance to keep Jimmy's wife in the address book and also a quick readiness to let go of the perpetual string of women, one by one, that he squired, some for a day, and some for eight years, like me, no matter how you felt about them. Not good to get too close to what was assuredly temporary.

Some were surprised to see Bella, my daughter, and me there at the service. Others knew Jimmy and I had remained friends, wrapped in a peculiar kind of friendship since the divorce, knew he and Bella always had a good-funny relationship, knew he had been invited to Bella's wedding (although too sick to attend). Some even knew that he had sent a lovely wedding gift to my daughter and her husband (a porcelain umbrella stand, Neiman Marcus, big bucks; I picked it out for him, but he had specified that the gift be an umbrella stand, for some odd reason. Bella loved it.). It was sad that so many of the couples we had known and done good stuff with now comprised just the men, standing there on the sidewalk, their stubborn wealth identifying them as rich and civil and smart. One wife was dead; three had Alzheimer's; and one was making funeral arrangements for a daughter who had just died of breast cancer. I thought three was a pretty big percentage of Alzheimer's for this group—four if you counted Jimmy's first wife. Then I didn't think about that. I thought about the difference in their looks from being sixty-five, which they were when I last saw them and which I was now, to being eighty, which they were now. Sixty-five is older; eighty is old, I thought. Then I didn't think about that any more, either. Life passes; people grow old. The bells began to toll and Bella and I had to go inside to sit in the front row.

I watched my daughter walk down the church aisle in front of me, tall, thin, shoulder-length dark hair, shoulders slightly stooped, elbows slightly protuberant as she moved forward, and I was overcome by how her posture seemed to reveal to me what I, in that moment, defined as her uncomplicated and determined moral center. She stripped away everything about Jimmy except the fact that he had been her step father for five years, had been mostly good to her, was probably crazy, and was now dead. That tie to him demanded that she take a role in his funeral--just a simple, straight-forward act, all potential complications erased. She was there for him and, a little, for me as well. Her enduring grace comes from that uncomplicated moral reliability.

The funeral seemed to go by very fast. The minister didn't say anything really personal about Jimmy—where to start—and just gave the generic more stately mansions remarks. Bella and I didn't feel out of place in the front row after all, not like fillers but really like part of the "family." I think the girls, Jimmy's daughters and grand daughters, were glad of our presence; we had always seemed incredibly stable people compared to poor wacky Jimmy and, to tell the truth, compared to the girls as well, who were by now mothers of their own daughters, one each, both with broken marriages behind them, both showing signs of the family bi-polar curse. They were beautiful girls, clear-skinned, blue-eyed blonds, and although now middle aged women, would always be *the girls* to me.

Their missing brother had not been located, last heard from in California. I had had some emails from him over the past several years and had given the last email address I had for him to them, but to no avail. I'm not sure he would have made an effort to attend the funeral even if someone had been able to find him. Of the three children, his was the most conflicted relationship with Jimmy and I don't think mental illness would have registered with him as an excuse for what he perceived as paternal abuse. I didn't know enough of the back story to have an opinion about Jimmy's parenting during the childhood years, but often watched Jimmy try to be the father-knows-best kind of father to his son who was, when I observed the relationship, a son who was now a man in his twenties being told to cut his hair, iron his shirt, sit up straight, make the putt. It was just so awful that Jimmy was so incapable of understanding how to be to him. And his son, blind to Jimmy's blindness, just chalked it up to brutality. We tell ourselves what we need to hear.

After the funeral, we all went to Jimmy's golf club— well, former golf club since he resigned when he moved to Florida—for cocktails and a buffet. It was a quiet party. I was able to talk with some people from our mutual past that I hadn't seen before the service and got more bad news, deaths, illnesses, a bankruptcy in one case, not the time of life when there is a hell of a lot of good news happening. But I was steadily amazed and somehow comforted by how really very nice all these people were, seen now from the distance of years, and how a troubled and silly man like Jimmy had been able to amass so many nice friends which I guess really did say a lot about his charm, his vulnerability, and his loyalty, because he *was* a loyal friend, America's Guest or not. I also realized how big a chunk of my life's memories were represented in this room. My marriage to Jimmy was an episode, a closed chapter, but it had meaning, I saw, had left meaningful connections. No matter how much we think we can erase connections, we cannot. One hour in company with the funeral guests let me see how bound I was to them, even if I would never see any of them again which, as I recall, after that day, I did not. Ties bind, memories hold, with or without presence. Every so often, I would hear news of their passing.

Bella and I finally just left. With promises to write, call, do lunch, whatever, we made our getaway and didn't keep our promises.

CHAPTER 2

One very dark night in St. Croix in January of 1988, when I was huddled on my bed, a twin bed next to Jimmy's twin bed, I knew that I was going to ask for a divorce and also that I was going to have to make love to him that night, soon. I was lying there, very tense, just trying to decide which to do. Knowing Jimmy, whichever one I did first (sex or end the marriage) would not preclude doing the other next; but because it was so dark and because we were leaving for home the next day, I decided just to make love to keep the peace and to tell him about the divorce after we got home, as I had originally planned. Jimmy had been extraordinarily crazy on the St. Croix trip and I think I felt a little frightened of him there, that night, alone in our very dark rental apartment by the sea, no moon, no external lights. Both of our daughters had been staying with us for a while during this vacation but, by now, on this dark night, they had both gone back to the States and we were alone. It's the only time I remember really being physically afraid of Jimmy's proximity in the whole time we were together, which is why I probably remember every detail of that night and of the days preceding it.

He had been quite nuts for almost the entire ten days that we were there vacationing on the island, especially nuts about his new compulsive project, buying property in St. Croix, and had been looking at some cliff-hanger lots located at a place called Carambola, a golf club resort enclave on the other end of the island from the apartment we were renting. There was some kind of story about Rastafarians coming out of the jungle fifteen years before, onto the verandah of the Carambola Golf Club and shooting (or was it hacking to pieces with machetes?) a dozen or dozens of guests while they rocked in their chairs and drank their gin and tonics. I never got the whole story from anyone either at Carambola or in Friedrichstaad. I was afraid to ask any of the natives since I was not entirely sure about the status of the alleged perpetrators and, naturally, this was not a subject the staff at Carambola was allowed to discuss, as one might imagine, not a tourism-promoter. The story did not seem to faze Jimmy. Like some, he thought any publicity was good publicity and felt, simply, that Carambola, actually called Fountain Valley at the time it was attacked, was "famous." Jimmy did not really acknowledge a significant difference between fame and infamy.

Many years later, I looked up the actual story of the Fountain Valley massacre and it was thusly told:

TRUE STORY: The Fountain Valley Massacre, St. Croix, USVI (*The resort is now renamed Carambola & boasts one of the best golf courses in the Caribbean.*)

Sept. 6, 2002 - St. Croix and the Virgin Islands were changed forever on the afternoon of Sept. 6, 1972, when the clubhouse of the Rockefeller-owned Fountain Valley Golf

Course was invaded by five masked men wielding shotguns, handguns and automatic weapons. Within a few minutes, eight people, including four tourists and two Rock Resort workers, lay dead, shot by the intruders, who then fled into the surrounding rainforest as suddenly as they had appeared. Eight more people, most employed by the golf course, were either shot at or wounded. For years, even decades, to come, what happened on that day would be a blight on St. Croix's image as a vacation destination.

Following by a day the slaying of Israeli athletes by Arab terrorists at the Olympic Games in Munich, the "Fountain Valley massacre," as it was quickly called, brought intense international media scrutiny to St. Croix as police, FBI and U.S. Marshals Service personnel initiated a massive island wide search for the gunmen.

Within a week, five African-Caribbean men, all native Virgin Islanders and at least one of them a Vietnam veteran, were under arrest. Charged with felonies ranging from robbery to murder, they were held without bail at the new Anna's Hope Detention Facility on St. Croix. The five -- Warren Ballentine, Beaumont Gereau, Raphael Joseph, Ishmael LaBeet and Meral Smith -- stood trial in U.S. District Court 10 months later. U.S. Attorney Julio A. Brady and Milton Branch, a federal prosecutor assigned to the case by the U.S. Justice Department, spearheaded the prosecution.

Brady would later run twice for governor, serve one term as lieutenant governor, and serve as a Territorial Court judge and as the territory's attorney general. A decade after the trial,

Branch would serve as commissioner of Public Safety (now Police) in the cabinet of Gov. Juan F. Luis. Heading up the defense were three mainland lawyers -- the celebrated William Kunstler and Margaret Ratner of New York and Chauncey Eskridge of Chicago. Kunstler was renowned for his association with activist political and legal causes, having defended the "Chicago Seven" after the riots at the 1968 Democratic National Convention and Native Americans arrested after incidents at Wounded Knee. Eskridge, a highly respected civil rights attorney, counted among his many clients the Rev. Martin Luther King Jr. and boxing icon Muhammad Ali. Court-appointed local attorneys Ron Mitchell of St. Thomas and Leroy Mercer of St. Croix rounded out the defense team.

Federal marshals James Macedon, a Crucian native, and Krim Ballantine, assigned by the federal government, supervised the tightly controlled federal courtroom in Christiansted's Government House. Krim Ballantine, who also had directed security at the "Chicago Seven" trial, is a St. Thomas resident today. After a lengthy pre-trial evidentiary hearing a dramatic, tension-filled trial, and a record-breaking jury deliberation, "The Fountain Valley Five," as the defendants had come to be known, were found guilty of eight counts of murder and multiple counts of assault and robbery.

Minutes after the verdict was delivered by a local jury, the five were sentenced by U.S. District Court Judge Warren Young to eight consecutive life sentences at mainland federal penal institutions. Within an hour, three Antilles Airboats whisked the five from the Christiansted waterfront to detention cells in Puerto Rico. A few days later, they were transported by the

U.S. Marshals Service to federal prisons in Georgia, Nevada, Indiana, Pennsylvania and Illinois.

The rumors were more entertaining than the factual version, especially the machete rumors. There were also some further extensions of the story, these concerning Ishmael La Beet, one of the perps (wonderful name, Ishmael La Beet – call me La Beet, ha-ha), a story that has him escaping captivity in the States and hi-jacking a plane to Cuba, but this lacks the ring of truth and is not often repeated in historic accounts of the massacre.

While I found the rumor sequence macabre, and much worse than the actual event that proved to be the ruination of Fountain Valley, a Rockefeller Resort, I could never fully shake the bloody image of the carnage while sitting and rocking on that same very beautiful verandah, sipping something, perhaps a gin and tonic. But alas, we Americans are all so inured to stories of death and bloody violence and universal hatred hearing about it daily as we do, that we can still sit there on those wide Caribbean verandahs and sip our drinks under the lazily twirling white fans, enjoying the view that we have paid well to enjoy, enforcing a very self-serving blissful ignorance of how much the world hates us.

Actually, the name "Fountain Valley" had been far more apt for the place—too bad the name got so blood-soaked—because the resort was located in a valley (surrounded by hills on which Jimmy envisioned building his future home and which he took to calling "my place in Carambola" before he even bought the lot), and because the valley was often under water. It was somehow proximitous to a tropical rain forest in the hills, thick with jungle-like foliage, so that at certain times of the year—apparently the time when we were there (and maybe always), it got brief but drenching rain storms three or four times a week. This left the golf course at Carambola soaked and a virtual mud hole as the water ran down from the hills and lingered in the valley. Everyone who played the course under these conditions, shortly after the rain ended, came back to the club house mud-spattered—players, caddies, other course employees. It was oddly amusing seeing everyone in such lush surroundings dressed in nice respectable golf clothing or resort uniforms looking so filthy and mud-caked. On the other hand, when you played the course on a sunny day between the rain days, the sun baked the course to a rock-like consistency and so it was sort of like playing down a paved road or off a rocky mesa. If you could get a club on the ball at all and get it even moderately airborne, the ball went a bloody mile, bouncing along and along, but it was not easy hitting off the cement-like surface, especially if you tried using a fairway metal. The only real benefit to playing in the sun was that your clothes stayed clean. For me, the course was a dud and unplayable, but it was one of the many things, like the massacre and the fact that he had little or no money with which to make this purchase, that Jimmy chose to overlook about his island in the sun. What he really liked was that they used American money and almost everyone spoke English.

At any rate, here I am lying in the bedroom on this dark, dark night, now just having had rather mechanical sex with my demented husband, just to keep the peace, you understand, to get out alive, when I muse silently that his daughter, or quite possibly his son (or both) metaphorically wanted to kill him. This wasn't a totally idle thought since at the airport, right before her premature departure, Christie had said to me: "I'm going to kill that bastard, and I might get Jimbo to help me because he hates him worse than I do." I know that "I'm going to kill him" is most often a figure of speech and not a death threat, but given the events that preceded Christie's early get away from the Crucian island in the sun, there was a more literal ring to the threat than was usual. But nothing about Christie's relationship with her father was even remotely "usual," and thus beggared speculation.

What prompted Christie's departure from St. Croix was this: Bella, my daughter, and Christie had stayed out late one night, allegedly clubbing in Christianstaad; well, in fact, they hadn't come home at all, Bella not until about four in the morning and Christie, Jimmy's oldest daughter, not until noon the next day. I was mildly annoyed because I was worried (remember the massacre!) and thought they should have called. They should have called, I said to Jimmy. But there was allegedly some problem with telephone service on the island after midnight. They said they had tried to call, but couldn't get through. Still. Jimmy, however, was sitting in a big hacienda chair in the corner of the apartment's living room, drinking something alcoholic, dressed in his white bathing trunks and matching jacket, red-faced and screaming, hysterically reacting to the girls' night out. With his long skinny bare legs and his eyes bulging, he looked like a huge praying mantis dressed in a white cabana set and also like some avenging father out of said 1950's TV show. He actually sent them to their room and, believe this or not, told them they were grounded. At the time, Bella, my daughter, was 25 and Christie, my stepdaughter, was 32, both with jobs and apartments of their own, so I remarked that he was probably mixing them up with some teenagers we no longer had as children and that a reaction appropriate to an adult might have been more suitable. His position was that if they acted like fucked-up teenagers he would treat them like fucked-up teenagers.

He really never came off that position and so when I went down to the bedroom after lunch, an hour or so later, to tell the girls that he might be more approachable by evening, Bella was asleep and Christie was packing. It was arresting to see her shoving everything into her duffle with such precision and such anger, both at the same time, blue eyes blazing, blond hair flying. She sat on the bed and told me she was leaving and asked if I could give her a ride to the airport. You're leaving now, I asked, and she said, yes, I called the airlines and changed my ticket and I'm getting away from that crazy bastard today. She was a beautiful woman, thin, real blond, slender nose, upturned mouth, lovely skin, always tense, always; and it seemed amazing to me that she could look that way after being up for more than forty hours. Later (much later) Bella told me she did coke. So she was beautiful, no matter, but also higher than the trees. How come I never figured any of these things out? How stupid was I or blind or just wanting the simplest answer vs. the more complex truth? I might just have been afraid of all of them. At any rate, I said sure, I'd drive her to the airport and when did she want to leave and she told me in half an hour. I wandered back out to the living room, distractedly looking out the big window at the pool and the beautiful turquoise Caribbean sea beyond. Jimmy was back in his hacienda chair reading the papers, local papers, real estate ads, mostly.

When Christie came banging out of the bedroom a half hour later, Jimmy said where the hell do you think you're going and she didn't answer, just pushed out the front door and headed for the car. She's going to fly home today, I said. Little change of plans, ha-ha. I'm driving her to the airport, I said. Like hell you are he predictably answered and ten minutes later we were all in our little rental car, headed to the airport, Christie stuffed in back with her duffle and big orange purse, Bella, rudely awakened from what had been her night's sleep jammed in next to her, me in the front passenger seat, and Jimmy still dressed in his little white cabana set, driving: Family portrait.

When we got to the airport and Jimmy tried to carry Christie's duffle inside, a duffle he had just rather roughly wrested from her grasp, she stalked ahead with her orange purse slung over her shoulder and ignored him. Just at that moment, an official airport guard, or whatever his job title was, walked up to us and said he couldn't let Jimmy inside the airport because, he said, Jimmy was not dressed appropriately. No little bathing suit inside, Mon, is exactly what he said. No bar legs. Jimmy went ballistic and almost got himself arrested protesting the guard's ruling on his cabana set (something Jimmy thought to be stylish and completely appropriate airport attire as well as pool wear).

We were eventually able to calm Jimmy down enough to get him back into the car. I told him to drive around the airport perimeter road and told him where to park and wait for us; and then Bella and I rescued the duffle and met Christie inside the lovely tropical airport, afloat in massive greenery and huge colorful blossoms, walking with her to her departure gate. We were all apparently dressed correctly (no little bathing suits, mon). Christie said that we should come home with her; then she said she was going to kill her father; and then her flight was called and she left. I noticed that some people were looking at us curiously, something I had almost gotten used to during the Jimmy years.

Bella looked at me as we walked back to find Jimmy and the car. She had that please-don't-even-start-the-conversation look on her face, but she had nothing to fear from me as I had no conversation to start. I probably could have asked where she and Christie had spent the night, but I didn't. I knew I would later discover or be told where they had been, sort of, and I did, nothing dramatic; but right now I was happy with my daughter safe and his daughter gone. I loved Christie, but I didn't think I could live through another minute of her fights with Jimmy or his fights with her and with luck, I wouldn't have to. I actually agreed with her spontaneous and anger-driven decision to fly away. It was the best choice. It was really going to be my choice as well, wasn't it? I mean, I knew this was the beginning of the end and that however long it would take for me to leave Jimmy, I would. Once started, it was a journey from which there was no turning back.

So as I lay there on my twin bed in our rented apartment on that darkest final night in St. Croix, knowing I would never ever come back to this island again; I was happy to be going home the next day. Bella had left, as she had planned, two days previously; Jimmy and I were packed. He was sleeping beside me after a short and mostly unsatisfactory sexual interlude. And I was a wife who was going home to end a marriage.

CHAPTER 3

I was convinced that I had tried everything, to save our marriage or to repair it, or to find some other way of being married. Perhaps I hadn't, but I was tired. I had read countless pages in books and on line about psychological factors that I thought might apply to Jimmy, to me, to our relationship. When I got to the point where everything I read seemed to fit him or me or us, I knew I was just projecting, too desperate for a solution, too short on psychological knowledge, too subjective. I don't even know now what propelled me to try; what (indeed) was worth saving?

There was, I think, a turning point, a specific day and time when I just gave up. It was in October, three months before our trip to St. Croix, and we had an infestation of flies in our house, an inexplicable congregation of black flies that nothing seemed to eradicate. One day they weren't there and then for days on end we had dozens of flies buzzing around, especially in the kitchen and dining room. We had a very clean and almost new house. We faithfully took out the garbage, did not leave food lying around, regularly sponged kitchen surfaces with anti-bacterial spray. The flies were a huge mystery. We did not think of ourselves as the kind of people who had flies. When bug sprays didn't work and I thought we'd expire from the chemical fumes they left behind, I went to the hardware store and bought some old-fashioned fly paper on the advice of the salesman. We were having a very warm autumn and the salesman said, reasonably, that the colder weather which would no doubt settle in any day would solve our problem, that flies had a short life span and wouldn't survive one cold snap. So I hung the fly paper in the kitchen, dining room and living room and prayed for cold weather.

Looking at the greasy brownish coils of waxy, sticky paper dotted with dead flies turned my stomach, reminded me of musty old grocery stores in the city of my childhood, but after a few days, the flies were far fewer and the outdoor temperature began to drop. I began to be hopeful. In the meantime, Jimmy and I had been planning a trip to Rome the following week with another couple and I started to focus on the trip with some faint notion that its anticipated and actual pleasures would breathe some much-needed joy into our relationship. The hope was slim but, irrationally, as the flies began to die and not re-appear, I somehow held on to that as some sort of talisman for hope in some vague corner of my mind.

Just a few weeks before, Bella had been home to attend a wedding with Jimmy and me. Frank, our friend, was a widower and had met a lovely woman, Nancy, a few years after his wife died. After a year they became engaged and now there was a happy, mid-life wedding planned. It was a family and close friends' affair and Bella wanted to be home for it. The wedding was at 5:30 PM on Saturday, a black tie event. About a week before, Jimmy had gallantly offered to pick up Frank's elderly aunt Rose, a woman he was fond of, and drive her to the wedding with us, but she declined, fearful that she'd want to leave the reception before we were ready to go. Jimmy assured her we'd leave when she wanted to—or take her home and come back, if need be, but she declined anyway. Jimmy said just to give a call if she changed her mind.

So, on the morning of the wedding day, Jimmy and I had fought about something that I don't remember. It may not even have been a fight but just one of those Jimmy-reaction things where something would piss him off and he'd slam out of the house without a word. He had done so that morning and left for his golf club (it was Saturday, after all) without a word about the wedding, what time we'd leave, or anything else relevant. As the day passed into afternoon, Bella and I got ready—took our showers, did our hair, and, finally, were dressed very nicely in our fancy wedding gear and sitting at the kitchen table, waiting, smoking, talking idly. It was a little before four and still no Jimmy. He will arrive home just in time, I said, and get ready without a word. We will have the twenty-five minutes it takes to get there and not a second more. That's his little game, I said to Bella, very calculated. Jerk, she said, as we continued to sit there. A little after four, the phone rang and it was Rose, saying she'd changed her mind and could we pick her up after all. Sure, I said, totally aware of what I was committing us to. See you soon.

At about four-twenty, Jimmy came in. He was doing his silent arrival act, heading for the bedroom when I said casually, Rose called. She wants us to pick her up. I don't need to narrate the rest of his manic whirlwind preparations, the seventy-mile per hour race to Rose's house, and our slightly late arrival at the church. His chagrin at almost breaking a promise to Rose and arriving late at our friend's wedding just to spite me made his anger even worse and, if he said two words to me during the entire ceremony or reception, I don't remember them. Bella left the wedding reception with other sons and daughters of friends, planning to spend the night at one of the girl's houses. Jimmy and I left with Rose, dropped her home, and then drove home in the perfect silence that now approached more than fifteen hours.

I still don't know how to describe this. I don't know how to say that this was one of dozens of times that I felt as if he'd opened my mouth and poured lead down my throat. I didn't know how one person who supposedly loved or in any way cared for another person could so totally erase her and demean her with such an uncivil, arrogant, and brutal weapon for so long. I tell myself now that he was possibly in some out-of-body world of horrific depression, fighting for his balance, a world in which I had no part and, thus, did not exist: Not guilty--by reason of insanity. I suppose an insanity defense has been used for worse sins.

And yet this kind of abuse (what would you call it: non-verbal abuse?) at the time seemed still not enough for me to leave the marriage. I had a very stubborn and blind determination for a long time to hang in and see where this marriage would go. I was not the divorcing type, I thought.

I was the loyal little terrier. After four years of a marriage more and more punctuated by these brutal incivilities, I still tried to understand and somehow to make it better. Do you want to know how I did this? Here's how: I read every *marriage advice book, column, psychological analysis* I could find, constituting a very long list. Every bit of advice was taken--from *give small gifts for no reason at all* to *give in if it's not important* to *keep your sex life exciting* to *seek counseling* to *a narcissist is wholly ego-centered and rarely effective in making meaningful commitments* to other well-meaning but useless information. I read them all and they all fit and I tried them all and nothing worked to change anything one little bit.

One day, Jimmy had called me at my office. I was in an informal meeting there with colleagues when the phone rang and I excused myself to answer thereupon to hear a string of obscenities and accusations blaring into my ear. It was my loving husband assaulting my soul while I tried to keep a straight face and not let on to the colleagues in my office that the screaming maniac on the phone was my husband, hoping against hope that the sound was not somehow leaking out of the earphone and into my office for all to hear. Somewhere in the middle of the diatribe I just said, I'll have to call you back on this. I'm in a meeting. I hung up and have no clue as to how the rest of my meeting went. My mind was just reeling. So, I guess there are times when silence can be the preferred mode of behavior.

At any rate, two months after the wedding silence (that actually lasted for the two days following the wedding, suddenly to be broken with normal chit-chat from Jimmy, as if nothing at all unusual had happened) and God knows how many other psychological brutalities, came the flies. I think of it always as "the flies," even though it was only marginally connected to them.

One morning, early, after about five days of fly paper and only a few living flies remaining, which I swatted dead, I decided to take down the fly paper. I couldn't stand it any more and I thought maybe the little beasts were just going away, as suddenly and inexplicably as they had come. I re-iterated my mantra: We are clean people. We do not deserve flies. Then I took the gruesome swirled strips down from the kitchen, deposited them in a plastic bag, and next took down the one from the chandelier in the dining room. I was balancing myself with one foot on the couch and the other on a glass-topped cocktail table in the living room reaching for the last of the fly paper hanging from the ceiling when I lost my balance, started to fall, tried to regain my footing on the table and, instead, put my foot through the glass. I was screaming as the table crashed over and there was blood from my foot all over the carpet. I raced to the kitchen to put my foot in the sink under running water, trying to pull out the little pieces of glass that were stuck in my foot and also trying, with paper towels, to stop the bleeding. Jimmy was theoretically still asleep down the hall in the bedroom.

During the next half hour, I got the bleeding stopped, put Bacitracin on all the cuts I could see, bandaged my foot, cleaned up the shattered glass, and then sponged the blood stains out of the carpet. I then hobbled down the hall to find Jimmy sitting up in bed, certainly very wide awake, reading something. He said: What happened? Nothing, I said. I fell, broke the table and cut my foot I added as I started to get dressed. Nothing else happened and you heard every last thing that did. And Jimmy continued to read. I think he might have said stupid—referring to me or to the fate that cut up my foot. It hardly mattered.

I was able to get an appointment to see a doctor who was also a friend later in the day. For some reason, I didn't want to see my regular doctor or to go and sit in the ER forever. My friend was a gynecologist, but agreed to treat my foot at his office, got the remaining glass out, took a few stitches, bandaged me up, told me how lucky I was to have missed the Achilles' tendon. He also told me to stay off the foot as much as possible for the next ten days and to come back in a week to get the stitches out. He never asked for details and all I told him was that I had fallen through the table. I didn't even mention the flies, the ostensible cause. I don't know what he thought. All I remember is what gentle hands he had.

Jimmy was preternaturally civil to me during the next few days, as I recall, as if trying to abide with great patience this little jerk of a wife who could be so stupid as to crash her foot through a glass table. But he went into a ballistic fit when I told him on the third afternoon after my fall to cancel our trip to Rome. All the time, I had thought it was very obvious. I couldn't get my foot into a shoe (was wearing flip-flops), couldn't walk without limping, had stitches that still needed to be removed, and could hardly embark on a Roman holiday, all things considered. His anger was unceasing and got even worse when I told him just to go on the trip with the other couple, without me. He came home one night stone faced and told me to get a note from the doctor saying that I couldn't travel so that he could get plane tickets and hotel deposits refunded. I did and he eventually got our money back and the silence abated after a ten-day stretch. But at some point during those ten days I was standing in the shower, trying to wash my hair while holding my bandaged foot outside the tub. It was awkward and frustrating and at some point I started to cry, something I rarely do. I'm not a crier by nature. But then the crying turned to sobbing and I was saying inside my head, over and over, I can't do this anymore. I've tried everything I know and I just can't do it. And I realized finally that I was talking to myself, not about washing my hair with an injured foot, but about my marriage. And that was that.

CHAPTER 4

Before we got married, Jimmy and I went around together for four years. I generally recall the events of those years, the ups, the downs, the silences or absences, the good times and good fun, the Giants' football games complete with tailgate parties in the parking lot or burgers in the Stadium Club, the trips to California or to the Caribbean, glamorous events like charity balls, casino nights, pre-some-award parties with his famous friends, all of these rather lumped together and vague, all in blurry bright colors, merged rather than distinct memories; but I do distinctly and clearly remember all the details of the single serious breakup that I thought would be final. We were engaged at the time and had been seeing each other for about three years. I was wearing a big diamond ring, a stone that Jimmy gave me that he had left over from some previous relationship or broken commitment and that I had re-set. This betrothal had been announced to friends, feted by co-workers, and they (and I) rather expected a wedding sometime in the near future.

I recall that it was late summer on a Sunday afternoon and that Jimmy and I had been out somewhere, that he had driven me home, and that we were sitting in his car in my driveway, just talking. The conversation was desultory until our talk turned to the upcoming wedding—or the alleged upcoming wedding, as it turned out. Even while Jimmy's proposal had been conventional enough—will you marry me, I'm sick of commuting, ha, yes, etc.—he now claimed that we both knew that our engagement was just a face-saving event for me to legitimize our relationship and our sleeping together to our children and friends, and that we really needn't think about marriage for a long, long while. We have bought your friends' good graces and made an honorable woman of you with this engagement, I remember him saying, so let's drop the wedding talk for now. In retrospect, I now know this idea was not original with Jimmy but was something adopted by many middle aged adults who were long-term dating, resisting marriage (for myriad reasons), and yet trying to define their relationships in conventional terms that other people could relate to and accept as "legitimate," since sleeping/living together was not yet accepted in any social strata. At the time, I just did not think of our engagement in those terms, nor had Jimmy ever described it to me as such--until this lovely summer Sunday in my driveway. So, it came as a stunning surprise.

I recall, however, that it was not even so much his words, cruel and shocking and unexpected enough as they were, in and of themselves, but more his tone that stunned me. While we had had our disagreements and fights, and traded insults in the past, he was using, there in his car in my driveway, a new tone that I had never heard before, totally without feeling, cold, disinterested. I looked at his face which was stiff, staring straight ahead at nothing and I felt as if I were talking to a stranger. He even looked a little different, older, thinner, I don't know. The more I tried to elicit responses from him that reflected some level of feeling, the more distant and estranged he became; and then suddenly he was blatantly insulting and accusatory in that new flat voice I barely recognized, until out of frustration and anger and pain, I took the diamond ring off my finger, threw it at him, and told him to fuck making an honorable woman out of me. I already was an honorable woman, no thanks to him. He said nothing. I went into the house and he drove away. At the time, I crazily thought this was just another fight. It'll blow over, I thought. Something in my rational thought process had obviously given way to wishful thinking of the deranged variety.

I recall that I subsequently instigated an awkward follow-up meeting on the following Saturday afternoon. He came to my house, presumably to talk over our situation, or at least that's what I thought or hoped for. I hadn't told anyone except Bella that we (or I) had broken the engagement, because I wanted to be sure that we really had. Apparently we had. Jimmy arrived at my house at the arranged time, rang the bell and walked into the foyer without waiting for me to answer the door, then sauntered into my large and sunny family room, sitting rather formally on the long couch to the side of the fireplace, the hearth filled with pots of white geraniums for the summer. At this little meeting I had asked for, he continued to sit formally, indifferently, as I tried to explain my anger, my failure to comprehend the idea of an "engagement of convenience," my very real commitment, my hurt, and the resultant flinging of the ring (for which I apologized and which he claimed not yet to have found in his car), me all the time searching for a way to reclaim or save the relationship, if that were possible. He made a few perfunctory comments signifying nothing and then abruptly got up and said something about plans for that evening and needing an exit line so he could just get the hell out of my house. He could have done nothing more persuasive than to act this way, like a bored ex-lover from some soap opera. So when he asked for an exit line, I said, here's an exit line; try *good-bye*. He smiled vaguely, said it, took a very deep breath, and left, striding out into the sunshine like a prisoner set free. I couldn't have been more crushed, more shocked, and more totally unaware of his motives than if he told me he were flying off to Katmandu for a year or two. I spent the rest of that weekend folded in on myself.

Following that brutal encounter, everything got very crazy. My friends knew (I told a few; they told others); I assumed his friends knew. People called me; most said I was better off without him (they were right). We were the scandal *du jour* for weeks. People asked me what happened and I said, quite honestly, that I didn't know, that apparently Jimmy understood that our engagement was bogus and enacted just for the sake of appearances, but that he hadn't managed to communicate that interpretation to me upon proposing and that I had, when informed, found it unacceptable.

I remember being devastated. I had been widowed for less than five years and I found myself coming close to that unbearable state of mourning, of endless pain, once again. I began to believe that I hadn't mourned the death of my dear first husband long enough, for less than a year when I met Jimmy, and that this was my punishment or my psychological payback. Oddly, I blamed Jimmy less than myself. He was just a re-bound lover for me, I told myself, or was it more of a re-bound obsession? I was the blind, stupid, selfish little bitch who just wanted someone in my life because I missed my first husband so desperately. My loss was so great that it truly was unbearable and I had stupidly sought to make it bearable by substitution, an act I now saw as sheer folly. I don't remember much else about those weeks. I got up, I went to work, somehow I must have managed to teach and attend to other school business, I came home, and I mostly hid out on weekends. I lost weight and felt as if my skin was stretched thin over my bones. Bella was away at college and knew only a limited version of the situation. I just couldn't bear a conversation with her that went into the details. A woman named Gretchen whom I knew mainly because she was dating one of Jimmy's friends oddly became one of my few confidants. She called me from time to time to update me on Jimmy's doings. He was dating a waitress, she thought. Great.

In fact, I started to get together with Gretchen on occasion, for a glass of wine or a meal at her house or a nearby restaurant, maybe because she was having a very tumultuous relationship with her own boyfriend, Jimmy's friend, George, and she thought we were kindred souls or something. We couldn't have been less kindred, to my thinking, but unlike my good friends, she didn't preemptively end every conversation about Jimmy with the phrase "you're better off without him." So I started meeting up with her every few weeks. We four--Gretchen and George, Jimmy and I--had gone out together a few times before my breakup with Jimmy and he and I also ran into them occasionally at local watering holes whereupon we often stopped to have a drink with them. Their relationship had always been volatile. George drank, heavily at times, cheated on Gretchen with an ex-girlfriend, and Gretchen was an aggressive woman who was more than happy to force any moment to a crisis. She let it be known that she took no shit, but then she took it. She and George had moved into a house together in my town so she now lived only a few miles away and I guess this was also why she sought me out from time to time. I know I chose to see her because she would always have some small bit of news about Jimmy and, painful as it was to hear, I (pathetically) still craved news. I will never, ever be able to explain this, to understand why, when let out of the cage of his insane affection, or lack of it, that I would want or need to get back into that cage. I know women do this all the time; I just didn't think I was the type.

One night Gretchen called me and told me she was breaking up with George, once again, finally and forever. He was up in the city for a few days on business which she had more than ample reason to believe was monkey business, seeing his old girlfriend who was allegedly seriously ill and in hospital, and when he came home, her plan was that he'd find her gone and the house devoid of all her belongings. She asked me to come over and keep her company while she packed. Later that night her brother, who was a state trooper nobody would want to mess with, was coming with a friend and a U-Haul to take all Gretchen's stuff away. It was all so ballsy and dramatic that I couldn't resist being there so dropped everything and drove on over. In truth, Gretchen was a beautiful woman, very dark and flashy, ribald and earthy. She looked like Sophia Loren in her hey day. She was younger than me and a lot tougher, but I really didn't know much about her history. I didn't think she had ever been married and knew she had no children. At this time, she was managing one of George's car businesses, but I had no clue as to what she had done for a living before that. I don't think I ever asked.

The house she shared with George was nice. It was on the inlet and the view over the marsh out to the water barely lit by the sunset red twilight was stunning. We sat out in two folding deck chairs on the expansive dock taking in the view and smoking cigarettes before the bugs started to get to us and we finally went indoors. I'm gonna miss that view, Gretchen acknowledged, but not what it costs my self respect. She had a point.

We drank wine and packed for two hours and had just about everything ready to go when we heard the front door open and just assumed that it was Gretchen's brother, on cue, come to take away the goods. Gretchen walked out to the foyer and I heard her say, holy shit, get the fuck out of here. Something in the middle of my chest tightened and I just knew, I don't know how, that it was Jimmy. Maybe he had said something or I just recognized the way he opened a door—crazy, but I had this instant need to get away. I sidled along the cabinets in the kitchen where we had been packing up the last of the dishes and glasses, opened the side door very quietly, and snuck outside, standing flat against the outside of the house next to the kitchen door, scared out of my mind for some reason or no reason. I then crouched and skittered across the back lawn and down onto the dock where I had a view back through the living room windows--but Gretchen and her company never appeared.

It was late September, but rather chilly on that particular night, and I was standing out there shivering in a sleeveless tee shirt and khaki shorts, but I wasn't going to move. I heard Gretchen's strident voice repeatedly telling Jimmy to get the hell out. I heard Jimmy laugh and say a few things I couldn't decipher and then I heard a third voice, a woman's, and I got more and more panicked, again for whatever reason. My car was parked out in the street so as not to block Gretchen's driveway, and there was a very good chance Jimmy had seen it there and wanted to come in just to torture me. Or maybe he had just come by to see George and my presence was a bonus chance to show off the waitress or whomever else he was with. My purse and car keys were still in the house or else I would have fled right then. Or maybe I wouldn't have because although I didn't have a name for what was happening to me, I was having what I'd later come to know was a full-blown panic attack. Blood rushed to my head, my hearing seemed to be dulled. My heart was jumping around, beating violently and irregularly. I really thought I was having a heart attack. Time telescoped. I stood there and stood there, fighting to breathe, one arm around a piling for support. Slowly my heart rhythms returned to normal and I was aware of Gretchen at the kitchen door, squinting through the dark to try see me, hissing at me, they're gone. The coast is clear, that bastard. I unclenched my fists realizing that my nails had dug into my palms leaving bloody little half moon imprints.

I followed Gretchen back across the lawn and into the kitchen and grabbed my glass of wine, draining it. He knew I was here, I said. Yeah, well he better not call George and tell him what he saw, Gretchen said. Well, he would if he could, I said, you know him, Mr. Gossip; but chances are George just might be incommunicado at the moment and, even if not, he'd never make it back here before your brother comes. At which opportune moment, in walked same brother with his buddy, two big, open-faced guys with buzz cuts and huge chests and big arms and we all started lugging boxes, furniture, wardrobes, suitcases, bedding, throw pillows, and other domestic appurtenances out to the U-Haul. The house, after we were finished, looked appropriately stripped, bared down to basic furnishings—couches, chairs, some nice antiques George had borrowed from his sister's antique shop—no signs of Gretchen left anywhere. I had to give it to her. It was all very masterful and in some strange and I'm sure sick way made *me* feel empowered, even though I was going nowhere, escaping nothing. By midnight, Gretchen was following the U-Haul driven by her brother down the street in her car and I was headed home in the opposite direction. I never did get the opportunity that night to find out who the woman was that Jimmy had brought with him and told myself that I didn't care, but when Gretchen called a few days later to give me her new telephone number (on penalty of death if I gave it to George or Jimmy or anyone),

I asked her who the woman was. Some slut, she said. I didn't know her, she added.

I don't think I ever found out who the woman was and memory tells me that the night at Gretchen's was the worst night of my broken engagement, primarily because of the frightening physical response I'd had out there in the dark on the dock, clutching the piling for dear life. Gretchen had moved herself far away from George to North Jersey and well outside of my geographical comfort zone that memorable night and so we saw little of each other following her departure. We'd call every so often over the next several weeks and then one day after a month or so of not talking at all, I ran into her at the local convenience store in town. She stood there in her jeans and tight black tee shirt, beautiful in no make up and messed-up black hair with a bag of potato chips and a bottle of Diet Coke in her arms, looking down at the floor, telling me that she had moved back in with George. I'm back with that fucking bastard is exactly what she said. I shrugged and told her you gotta do what you gotta do. You might say that was the end of my ur-friendship with Gretchen.

Sometime shortly after that encounter, I went to visit a long-time friend of mine, Eileen, who lived on a farm out in the country, inland and away from all the little shore towns my other friends and I inhabited. It was a place of beauty and peace and silent acres, trees, a brook, birds feeding at the dozen feeders hung from the trees around her dark green farmhouse, her pool in a field adjacent to her house, a pool which she called her one indulgence. She loved to swim in its icy waters. She lived alone with an army of cats in varying stages of domestication. We had worked together at the college until she retired to her farm, but we remained close friends. She was old enough to be my mother and maybe I treated her that way a little. She had heard a lot of Jimmy stories from me over many months, hated him profoundly because, first, he was just the sort of person she would hate and then, ultimately, because she detested what he had done and was doing to me and, worse, that I was letting him do it. I walked into her farmhouse, through the cluttered porch/ anteroom, filled with cats sleeping in various sunspots, on shelves or on old cushions, and into the kitchen where I poured myself a cup of coffee from the pot that always had coffee, and sat down at her kitchen table cluttered as usual with the dozen or more catalogs she always kept there, *LL Bean, Jackson and Perkins, The British Museum, Antiques Today*: The catalogs changed, but there were always several and each represented important pieces of Eileen's varied if solitary life. I really adored how she lived, how elemental she and her life were. Wild, domestic, intellectual, plain, lonely, alone, yet so full, cats and dogs, friends, every day, every corner of her house and life, so full and yet still so neat.

Just as I was settling in with my coffee at the cluttered table, Eileen came in from the other entrance into the kitchen, through a Dutch door that led to a small covered brick terrace and side garden where we had sat on many a lovely evening with wine and snacks and cigarettes. She had an armful of Mums ablaze in late fall colors and said she had seen my car come up the road from the garden but knew I could find coffee while she finished harvesting. She buried her face in the Mums and commented on their acrid smell. She took some vases from a shelf above the very old fashioned farm sink and began making large and small arrangements, snipping stems and sorting colors as she went efficiently about this business of bringing autumn inside, as she put it. She was a small, neat woman, still blond, filled with the kind of compact energy that enlivened her serviceable clothing, L. L. Bean, most likely, and animated her unlined and intelligent face. I think it was this plain and visible energy about her that most reminded me of my own mother who had died many years before.

I loathed having to talk to her about Jimmy, always feeling apologetic about my demented attachment and willingly-accepted debasement. But I wanted to talk about my physical response to his showing up at Gretchen's house. I wanted someone to tell me that I wasn't crazy or to go get an EKG or to buy a farm. I don't know. But whatever, it was during that conversation that Eileen and I determined that I should see a shrink. Maybe long overdue, I conceded. I knew Eileen would talk to me endlessly but as she so rightly pointed out, it was all just repetition. She had nothing new to say. And in the end, after all the talk, she still didn't get it and I didn't either; but both of us wanted me to get it. She actually knew someone I could see whom she recommended. She knew this woman, the shrink, Dr. Waxman, socially, distantly, and said she was sensible, whatever that meant and however that bore on being a good shrink. But I was going to call her. I left a few hours later, after a walking tour of the farm, around many of Eileen's beautiful ten acres, the walking a ritual we often performed, just looking at what was growing, even at the end of October. I was full of coffee, good advice, and maybe just a little hope,

hope for myself. Somehow, when I was with Eileen, I could imagine a life without Jimmy. It somehow seemed feasible and even, more importantly, desirable.

So I called Dr. Waxman's office and made an appointment for the following week. She turned out to be a comfortable woman of about sixty, grey-haired, plump, and nicely dressed. I had nothing to compare her with, novice to the shrink world as I was, but I liked her. This was in the eighties and people still thought people who saw shrinks were crazy, although definitions of crazy kept changing. I would, however, have admitted to any kind of crazy where Jimmy was concerned or would have at least conceded, as I did to Dr. Waxman, that my behavior concerning him was far from rational. Dr. Waxman pointed out, in turn, that emotional relationships were rarely rational but that did not mean that they needed to be destructive—and on that point we launched our long, long series of conversations, very few of which I remember precisely. I did most of the talking, but I found her silences, her questions, and her relatively few comments comforting. I can say that I think she gave me perspective or allowed to me discover it for myself. I can say that for at least a while, I was able to set certain parameters (this I will not tolerate; this I can overlook). I can say this worked. And I can also say that after all the things that happened--in the time between seeing Dr. Waxman and initiating my divorce--I was finally able to circle back, five years later on that desperate day in the shower with my tears and my poor injured foot, to the point where I knew with absolute certainty that *this*, meaning by then my entire marriage, this I truly *will not tolerate*.

CHAPTER 5

We were driving someplace far away, Florida, maybe, or Charleston, in Jimmy's big white Cadillac, the miles on Interstate 95 rolling smoothly beneath us. We had been talking and the conversation began to lead in an indirect way toward the previous end of our relationship, and now, after three months of tentative connections, its reconstruction, if not necessarily its total repair. And then Jimmy said oh no; you are not going to sit there and lecture me while I'm trapped behind the goddamned wheel of this car and can't get away. My former wife used to do that—he didn't specify which former wife—and it's never happening again. I know all about that little game. I didn't answer. One of my new-found strategies, in a phrase I had learned from Dr. Waxman, was not to take the bait. In my head I was thinking: *I'm not lecturing and I'm not your ex-wife*. But like a stubborn little fish swimming on past the baited hook, I just turned and looked out the car window as if the scenery alongside Route 95 was fascinating. I shifted my knees slightly to point toward the passenger door and I could feel the atmosphere shift, or at least *my* atmosphere shift, and saw his words break up like fading smoke in the silent air inside the car. This was not so much a strategy on my part or even a retreat as much as it was a control mechanism, imagistic, a form of self-assertion, a silence not dignifying the comment with a response. But it wasn't even the traditional abusive silent treatment, as I was willing to talk again—now or later. I was just not willing to talk about that subject, whatever it was, the bait thing. It was just an act of ignoring, pretending I hadn't heard the last remark—or had heard but had chosen to take neither offense nor defense. I found this had been working for me, especially since I taught myself not to care what he thought or might be thinking or what he either was or was not saying.

I remember looking over at him, a very tall man, clean beyond the norm, fine features, elegant of posture, his hand draped gracefully over the steering wheel, his silver hair reflecting light, a man so full of physical grace and so lacking in psychological grace that I felt tears start to come to my eyes.

It may well be that I knew all along that Jimmy just wasn't normal, knew it in an existential way. I mean, I know no one is *normal* but it just might have occurred to me at that moment, more specifically, that he was a man trapped in his own pain, in his own inability to do human emotion in the way that most people instinctively know how to do it. There were things missing in him that no matter what he tried, he couldn't replace because he didn't even know what they were. And of course I had to put those thoughts away. If I chose not to respect and respond to his words, and I think I was beginning to, could I also see and tolerate him as someone with essential parts missing, parts I could never find for him? And yet, seeing this absence, could I still stay with him? As I thought these things, he actually grew dimmer to me, quite literally looking physically blurry. I shook my head and made a joking comment about a Stuckey's billboard and we started talking again, about things you see south of Washington that you don't see north of it on I-95 and, for the moment, my impossible question, spoken silently to myself, went unanswered.

We had resumed seeing each other, casually, in late winter and, eventually, had gotten re-engaged in the spring. I think it happened because Jimmy got tired of the waitress (or whoever she was) and he discovered that I had started dating other men. But it happened dramatically, of course.

I had been out with a few men starting about Christmas time, one person I worked with, a relationship which was going nowhere, and another man from town who, I think, was using me as his re-bound person. He certainly was using me for something. I might have been interested in him if he had found a way to look at me when we were out for dinner instead of looking over my head at every other person in the room. I was also fixed up by a well-meaning girl friend with a very good looking older man whom, I later found out, was a drunk working on his third DWI, riding his bike to the supermarket and hitching rides from anyone handy. I ran into him one night at a local restaurant, a long time after we had stopped dating, and he actually asked me for a ride home--which I gave him, no hard feelings. After the New Year, I got fixed up again through mutual friends, this time with a man from out of town, a big-firm New York lawyer, recently divorced. He lived in the city but the plan for our first date was that on the appointed Saturday, he would visit his mother in Rumson for lunch and then continue down the shore to meet me and take me out for dinner. He came well-advertised--handsome, intelligent, sophisticated, graduate of Princeton and Yale Law School, big career going. What's the saying: If it sounds too good to be true, it probably is?

He arrived at my house for this first meeting, a nice-looking man as advertised, medium everything (height, weight, hair), dressed nicely, looked a little bit like a young Jack Lemon. He was pleasant initially. I offered him a drink and he readily accepted, requesting vodka on the rocks. He quickly finished the drink, asked for a second, and, finishing that in even less time, said wow the drinks really flow like glue in this place and went into the kitchen to make himself a huge third refill (I was guessing he'd had about twelve ounces of vodka in less than half an hour). I got the picture. I was about to spend the evening with yet another drunk. Great. The people who fixed me up with him were really nice and very good friends so in deference to them, I didn't want to just tell this man to go, or that I didn't like drunks, or that I suddenly had a big headache. I thought unreasonably that maybe things might get better.

Fortunately, he let me drive his car to the restaurant. You know how to get there he said and I don't want to spoil the ride listening to all that turn here stuff. And if you're anything like my ex-wife, you don't know right from left anyway, ha-ha. Why this epidemic suspicion by men that you're "like" the ex-wife? Why do people talk about "women" as if we are all identical? I consider this type of generalizing to be a basic index of gross, paranoid stupidity. Once at the restaurant, my drunken date slipped the *maitre de* five dollars for the best table (which we didn't get), flirted with the waitress, ordered a vodka martini up (no rocks; serious drinking now), ordered one for me, too, and then ordered dinner for both of us. The lady will have. He did let me select the temperature for the huge steak he ordered for me of which I ate little, which he noted (appetite like a bird; no wonder you're so skinny). Sadly, the restaurant had a band and after dinner, he insisted we dance, something he could not do (surprise) but of course thought he could, better than John Travolta in *Saturday Night Fever*, using the whole dance floor in the process to the distinct displeasure of others trying to use the dance floor, too. I had two thoughts. Thank God I don't know anyone in this restaurant and thank God we'll be leaving soon and I'll never have to see this man again.

I drove again on the return trip and as we got closer to my house he asked if there was any local action, any place we could go for a decent drink. I didn't get the point of the question since for him a decent drink was straight vodka and he'd already had enough of that to float a battleship, but in the mood for not pissing him off and avoiding one of those horrible irrational un-winnable confrontations with drunks who are always right, and so long as he was willing to let me drive, I dutifully drove to a little club I knew. It was owned by and styled after a popular Manhattan club and it must have pleased him because we sat at the bar for about an hour while he surprised me by switching to Rusty Nails, a drink made from scotch and Drambuie, more straight booze.

He used his drinks-flow-like-glue line with the bartender who just looked at the wall and spaced the refills. I wasn't drinking anything by this time, so full of water and club soda that I thought I'd burst, but my considerate date didn't seem to notice. He was waving at some woman across the bar who was studiously ignoring him—and then suddenly it was last call and time to go and so we did.

What I didn't know at the time was that Jimmy was somewhere in this club at the same time as we were, saw me and my wonderful date, and then proceeded to follow us home. He then stood in my back yard looking through my family room window. I had no idea about any of this at the time, but it is an important part of the story that you need to know.

When we got home, my date followed me into my house and requested that I make some coffee for him before he "hit the road," and while we sat in the family room waiting for the coffee to brew, he started (no big surprise) to put the make on me. This man was just one big collection of tedious clichés. By this time he was definitely in stumble-bum territory and I thought I could just push him off pretty easily, but suddenly he was pretty strong and pushing me down onto the couch and trying to kiss me, missing my face and sloppily kissing my throw pillows and then my hair instead. The more I pushed, naturally, the more assertive he became and just when I thought I might really be in some kind of trouble, someone started ringing my front doorbell like crazy, repeatedly. My wannabe lover was startled enough that I was able to push out from under him and get to the front door, opening it to find Jimmy on the doorstep. Who I expected to find at two-thirty in the morning, I don't know, but the Craig's List killer would have been preferable to my date at that point. Jimmy pushed his way into the family room and asked my date who the hell he thought he was and to get out. My date in turn asked who Jimmy thought *he* was and then they started a pushing match that quickly became a kind of fist fight. Jimmy had clearly had a few drinks, but my date had had about a gallon of booze, so there was really no contest (and Jimmy was a lot bigger). I think Jimmy landed a few punches and then my date just grabbed his keys and ran out the door into his car. I had one second of guilt about him going off into the night with other drivers on the road and all that booze in his brain while the coffee still brewed in the kitchen, but there was no help for it. And I did want him gone.

Not my best date, I mumbled to Jimmy. He just stood there for a minute, asked if I was OK, and then left. I cleaned up after the fight—a toppled lamp, a spilled ashtray, some stray throw pillows. And then went to bed feeling like someone out of a bad movie, and far too old for what had just happened.

Things only got worse. At about nine AM the next morning I was awakened by a telephone call from my charming date, raving like a lunatic, insisting that I identify Jimmy so that he could call the police and get him arrested for assault. He also told me that he was going to sue me for aiding and abetting. I asked him to suspend all action, that I would put him in touch with my lawyer in the hopes that we could work things out amicably. Understanding that the guy was probably still drunk (was he ever sober?), I didn't have a lot of faith in his rational judgment (especially since he said he had a black eye and abrasions on his jaw); but since he wasn't entirely blameless, since I guess I could have charged attempted rape for which I had a (peeping Jimmy) witness, I thought I held some cards. I didn't say any of this to avoid enraging him further and he finally agreed to give me an hour before he called the local police to file a complaint. I called my lawyer, Gabe, at his home and discovered from his wife that he was on the golf course, so I called the club and asked them to get him to call me, that it was an emergency.

My poor lawyer had to leave the golf course and listen to every detail of my predicament (and I spared none) over the phone as his golf partners awaited his return to their game. I was truly mortified by the telling of my tale of woe, but did believe the lunatic date really would call the police if we didn't do something. My lawyer agreed to call the nut and whatever they talked about seemed to work as the nut himself, also a lawyer, called me back and revised his plans. If I were willing to pay his alleged medical bills, he'd drop the matter. I readily agreed, saying that was totally fair, you betcha, absolutely, send them here; but, as it turned out, I never got a bill and never heard from the guy again. When my friends who had fixed us up asked me a few weeks later how the date went, I just said that we weren't really a fit, but thank you anyway. Later, my lawyer told me he had played the sympathy card--young widow, young daughter, small town, have a heart (not totally saturated by vodka). Maybe my lawyer didn't tell me everything. Maybe there was a subtle suggestion of attempted rape charges and the vulnerabilities of big-firm lawyers. I'll never know.

The outcome of this strangely affected my thinking about the break with Jimmy. I wasn't sentimental enough to believe he had been my hero, although in a small way, he had been (God knows how far the drunk intended to go to "have his way with me"). But I did begin to believe that mid-life relationships all came with enormous baggage, baggage that my little experiences that winter in the world of middle-aged dating had revealed and that Jimmy was, in some ways, the devil I knew. He rarely drank to excess (it made him ill), had never shown any inclination toward physical violence and, as he had tried to persuade me, he was really trying to save me from *himself* when he broke up with me. He said he was a philanderer and a screw up and that I deserved better. This is probably an ancient defense, too, and was almost beside the point, but it looked to me like a starting point from which we might find a way forward. My shrink didn't disagree, and I kept talking to her about those parameters and got better at defining them and dealing with them, at not taking the bait, and then finally, finally used all of this in the end, ironically, as the basis for my divorce. It took five years, but sometimes I'm an incredibly slow learner.

CHAPTER 6

When we got married on June 10, we did so in a small, anonymous church vestry in the city, with Christie and Bella as our witnesses, followed by an extravagant champagne lunch at the Tavern on the Green for just the four of us. A friend loaned us his apartment in the Manhattan House for our honeymoon or whatever one calls those days after the wedding when the bride and groom are over forty, and so we did New York things--theater, clubs, shopping, extravagant restaurants, once meeting Jimmy's friends, a celebrity couple, for dinner. It was a good time. I had sold my house in May, put a lot in storage, and Bella and I and our old dog and cat moved into Jimmy's two-bedroom apartment in his high-rise on the beach at the shore, several miles north of my home town.

I liked the apartment well enough. It was light and spacious floating above the world in its concrete tower and I had spent a lot of time there prior to the wedding, but I didn't like the life style it imposed on me. As Bella put it, you have to put on your earrings to get the mail. When you wanted your car, you had to call the valet and wait until he got around to fetching it (or trudge through the spooky dark parking garage to get it yourself). The garden was two planters of red geraniums on the deck and a fichus tree in the living room. We had to take the dog down in the elevator to walk her on what we called poo path. She was an old dog by that time and didn't need much exercise, but the trip down the elevator, especially if we had company on the ride, was terrifying for her and sometimes her aging kidneys couldn't make it to poo path and so we also had to carry mop-up supplies in case she had an "accident." I felt constrained, felt that too much of my life was visible to strangers--the unknown neighbors, elevator companions, the building's staff--and was eventually able to extract a promise from Jimmy that we'd look for a house and move as soon as we found one.

I know Jimmy didn't want to move. He thought the apartment was sophisticated and low maintenance and fit his self image. It did have advantages: Proximity to the beach, two nice restaurants across the street we could walk to, a very nice outdoor pool-lounge area, tennis courts, and a lovely location surrounded by water with great views. Unquestionably it was in the high-rent district and provided a distinctive and recognizably prestigious address. But it remained for me after a year of living there as just a nice place to visit, never home. Jimmy had fixed me up with a realtor, a long-time friend of his, and the plan was for the realtor, Betty, and me to scout available properties and then, if we saw anything worthwhile, to arrange for Jimmy to see it. Meanwhile, Bella got a job as a waitress for the summer at one of the restaurants across the street, made friends, and seemed not to mind the relocation. She would be returning to college in September, so this time for her was summer fun, or so I thought. I'm sure there were complex emotions that Bella chose not to share, but she was pretty good about discussing the practical issues of our living arrangements and I think we all adjusted as the summer went on, each of us at least trying to accommodate the needs of the others while having our needs accommodated as well.

Jimmy was remarkably affable and peaceful during the first year of our marriage. He was more considerate than I'd ever known him to be, took pleasure in introducing me as his "wife" to people I hadn't met, and he really seemed to want to settle into domestic living. He still spent most of every Saturday at his golf club, golfing or playing poker or both, but we almost always went out for dinner on both Friday and Saturday nights and occasionally during the week. On Sunday, mid-mornings, we went to a local breakfast place on the beach and spent an hour or more eating big breakfasts, talking, reading the Sunday *Times*. From time to time, when she didn't have to work, Bella came with us. Many Sunday afternoons the two or three of us went to the pool, if Jimmy and I weren't playing golf with friends, came back up to the apartment to watch golf on TV, and then had our inevitable hamburgers for dinner. During the week, Jimmy worked, but because I was off for the summer, I was free. I shopped, played golf at my home club where I retained my membership with the regular Tuesday group and joined a Thursday group at Billy's club. Often, I went back down to my town on Saturdays to play golf in the afternoon with a long-standing foursome. I also spent some time making adjustments to the apartment to better accommodate three occupants.

Given the turmoil of the years leading up to this union, this year was nothing short of remarkable. I was almost consistently happy. It seems incredible to me now.

I often wonder if I had just been willing to give up almost all contact with my previous life and my need for a house and had remained Jimmy's little princess in his tower, if all this happiness would have continued. I guess every partner in an unsuccessful marriage thinks about this. If I were to have given up very meaningful parts of me and just been exclusively what he/she wanted me to be, would it have been worth it? Obviously, the answer is almost invariably no. We are what we are; we need what we need; we have histories; few of us surrender to personal obliteration easily, if at all. And if we do, the inevitable result is still disaster, albeit a different kind of disaster. So no. We had a great year but in order for it to continue, I would have to have vanished into some new iteration of myself. Still, it was nice year.

We found a few attractive houses in towns that neighbored our apartment and came close to buying one until we found ourselves in a bidding war (the attractive sale price proved indeed too good to last). Jimmy was incensed by the competitive bidding and pulled us out. It really was a lovely house and I was disappointed but fully agreed that it was getting a bit rich for our blood and heaven only knows where the top price would get to. After that, I parted ways with Betty and got a new realtor whose territory was to the south of the county, the area where I used to live. I thought that prices might be more reasonable there, that it was not that much further from Jimmy's office in drive time, and that I'd get back "home." I missed my town and proximity to my friends. And I was sick of the long drive to the college from the apartment (an hour each way). For whatever reason, Jimmy did not object to this shift of venue at the time and we eventually found a house in the town that I had moved away from to marry him two years before. In fact, it was not a house that I would have chosen on my own, lacked that magic word, "charm." But it was relatively new and spacious, well-priced, and on a nice lot. Jimmy thought it was a great deal price-wise and because he had found something terribly wrong with almost every other house we had seen and actually said he liked this one, I bought it.

In line with our pre-nuptial agreement that we would not have any "joint property," I agreed that because this house was in my town and the place I'd live if we ever got divorced, it was best if I "owned" it. Jimmy retained ownership of his apartment in the tower and rented it out. I don't remember ever feeling particularly proprietary about the house I bought that I barely liked, only that it was "fair" that I be the owner. But over the next few years I would learn that Jimmy resented my ownership, *my* house in *my* town, accusing me of acting like the queen bee ever since we moved into the house. Maybe I did act that way, God knows. I never felt that way, I know, but did do a lot of work with the house, hiring a decorator for the first time in my life and also a landscaper. Maybe I actually was just a little too house proud to be around, relieved to be away from the constraints of the apartment, happy to be back in a town that had always felt like home to me, but because I didn't really love the place, I tend to mistrust that view.

I was just trying to get more comfortable with the house, create something relatively charming and livable for us all. This may have come across to Jimmy as preening; it may have reminded him of my independence; he may have felt horribly dislocated and disempowered. Whatever, I was no longer the little princess in the tower; I was the landlady, and although I didn't see it, the marriage was essentially over the day we moved into that house. That it took another three years to expire was just the long end of the inevitable; but one never sees the inevitable. Were we to see it, we'd re-write the plot.

It was during this time that I noticed Jimmy starting to flirt outrageously, most notably with women who were part of the various groups we would dine with on Saturday nights, married women, wives of friends, women whom he had professed previously to dislike, all were suddenly objects of his very close attention. He'd sit next to them, drape an arm around the back of their chair and lean in close to talk to them, effectively blocking me out of the conversation if I were sitting on the other side of him. He would come home from work with constant stories about Debbie, the head trader at his investment office, talk about how pretty she was, how he even thought he'd like to sleep with her. He flirted with waitresses when we were out for dinner alone and suddenly found a few non-descript neighbors totally fascinating. I put all of this, every stupid second of it, into the don't take the bait category. I knew it was all aimed at me, and I just refused to respond. There were times when I thought to myself--go ahead; you want him, he's all yours, but of course no one would have been crazy enough to want him. He was always and ever all mine.

But then one night, just like that, it got to me. We were at my club for dinner with a group of my friends. It was a dinner dance and Jimmy had been doing his close-talk thing with a woman with whom I was not particularly friendly, friends of friends who had joined our party. She had some sort of emotional problems, I had heard, and she always seemed very nervous and edgy whenever I encountered her which was not very often, maybe occasionally in the supermarket or at the drug store.. She was rarely on my radar. At one point in the evening, all the couples at our table were dancing except for this woman, who sat there, her husband having wandered off to the bar. She was confiding to Jimmy how she was a secret smoker. Her eyes seem to bulge as she spoke. Her husband would kill her if he knew she smoked, she said, so she went into the bathroom to smoke, totally naked to keep the smell off her clothes. Jimmy picked up on the naked part, and the woman who appeared quite drunk to me, was sort of gurgling and saying, yes, totally naked, not a stitch. Just as I was going to ask her about the smoke smell on the towels, I sort of snapped. Instead of joking it all along, I asked her to get the hell away from the table, that I needed to talk to Jimmy privately. She looked at me as if I were from another planet; but eventually she got my message and wobbled away from the table on her too-high heels.

Then I said to Jimmy: Do I have your attention? This is the end of this game. You can flirt with whomever you want, but not when I'm at the table or in the room. You can sleep with whomever you want and if I catch you, I'll divorce you. But you will *never* again embarrass me with this absurd and infantile behavior. Am I clear? Now I'm going to the ladies room and when I come back, I want a mature and civil husband sitting at this table.

I fully expected him to be gone when I got back, but he was not and for whatever reason, the flirt game was over and seemingly for good, as it worked out, with only a few hour's worth of his pouting after my little speech. When I look back on it, I am almost certain that the flirting was some sort of warped coping strategy that Jimmy had devised in his twisted and agonized mind, a strategy to cope with what he saw as my "queen bee" attitude about my house and, I suppose, about our marriage which, as he chose to perceive it, was now on my territory. As I also recall, this was one of the few times, perhaps the only time, that I ever gave Jimmy an ultimatum, so perhaps something in him sensed I would act on what I said.

He would develop other strategies designed to retrieve power in our relationship, power that he imagined he had lost, the power he had once felt he owned as he was strutting around in his luxury apartment and its surrounds, summoning valets, bullying other employees, power he sensed that he had lost when he moved into "my" house. But none of his tactics worked with me ever again because what he had really lost was not his power, but his mystique. Thanks to Dr. Waxman, I could see him relatively clearly, could identify tactics as tactics and thus no longer be hurt by them and, unhurt, I was a far more dangerous adversary.

Janet Hubbs

I'm not sure Jimmy ever could or would articulate this for himself and I never defined or wanted to define our relationship in terms of power, but I see now that Jimmy in his own crazed way truly was a man of the 50s; that everything was about power: Me Tarzan, Father Knows Best, Man's World, Woman's Place, Men Rule. And not only did he have a woman, me, who thought all that was shit, it was something for which he was totally and absolutely unfit. Because underneath it all, he just wanted a mother. He wasn't Tarzan; he was Boy.

CHAPTER 7

I got sick while we were married. The main symptom was an arrhythmic heartbeat that scared the hell out of me. All my life I had had missed beats, a jumpy heart as I called it, diagnosed as a benign murmur or premature ventricular contractions by several doctors seen over the years, and eventually I got used to the inevitable skipped beats that I would experience as a sense of panic, a little bird trapped in my chest beating its little wings to get out. Somewhere in there one of the doctors I had seen for this condition tied it to stress, but by then "stress-related" applied to every disease known and unknown to man, so I shrugged this off. My belief is that anxiety is part of the mortal coil, for some more than for others; for me, big time. Unwilling to take anti-anxiety drugs, I had pretty much decided to "live with" my hasty heart until one night during our first summer in the new house.

Christie, Jimmy's daughter, was visiting us and we had had the usual share of sniping and verbal battles between her and Jimmy, but no more than usual--possibly a little less as Christie, Bella and I spent some pleasant time shopping or at the beach during the weekdays. Our house and its location offered little excitement for Christie, however; no big go-go bars to visit or guys to troll for.

Then one night during this visit, in the small hours, I was awakened with heart palpitations that were very intense and just would not go away as they usually did. Early in the AM, I asked Jimmy to take me to the emergency room because I was scared. We went and then endured all the ER could dish out in terms of aggravating delays and miscues. I finally told Jimmy to go home as he was jumping out of his skin with impatience. I said I'd wait and call him when I knew anything. At about noon, they decided to admit me for observation and after getting settled in my hospital room, I called Jimmy who was now at work and told him I'd be spending the night at the hospital. Bella was away for a few days and I didn't want to worry her so postponed calling her until after I got home. I called Christie who was still at the house but she was out, so I left a message. As the afternoon wore on, I had a battery of tests and needle sticks but was told I'd have to wait to see the doctor in the AM to get results.

So I watched bad TV, ate my bad hospital dinner, and then must have dozed off in my narrow hospital bed because the next thing I knew, it was about 7:00 PM and I woke to see Christie and Jimmy at the foot of my bed, laughing and saying wake up, wake up! Are you alive? What dawned on me first was how cheery they were, how beautifully healthy they looked, how unusually compatible they seemed, and that they may have had a cocktail or two before the visit. My heart thumped. I told them I didn't know anything, would see the doctor in the AM, felt a bit better, palpitations calmed down somewhat. They seemed only mildly attentive, looking around, out the window, until Jimmy finally said, well, let's get out of here, Christie. I hate hospitals and I want to go get some dinner. Oh, right, I said, dinner. You two must be starved. Go get some food! They left and I noticed that it was twelve minutes after seven. Somewhere my brain logged the fact that they'd been there for maybe eleven minutes. After they left, the lady in the next bed asked if that had been my husband and when I said yes, she said he's very handsome. I may have said handsome is as handsome does, but I doubt it.

I got out of the hospital equipped with a new doctor, a cardiologist, and some pills, beta blockers, tranquilizers, and some other drug I don't remember. I also got a lot of assurances that this was nothing to worry about, that there was no heart pathology. I wondered why, if not, I was taking these pills. But anxious to believe that I had a healthy heart, I took the pills and did feel better. The tranquillizers were only for use "as needed." Take one, lie down for an hour and if the heart doesn't calm down, take another. If it doesn't calm down after another hour of rest, call the doctor.

I thought at first that maybe I had just been doing too much. We had moved into the house in May, with all the tedious sorting, packing, unpacking, re-sorting and storing that this entails. Some of Jimmy's stuff went into storage, most of mine came out, and naturally we wound up with some rooms partially furnished, a few not furnished at all. Old furniture never fully does it for a new house. We furnished the house with "his" and "mine," but no "ours," as per our pre-marriage financial arrangement: No joint property. So if we needed something new, one or the other of us had to buy it. Since Jimmy's attitude had already started to become defensive about "my" house, he was not particularly enthused about making any purchases, so except, as I recall, for a television set, I bought just about everything else. Since Jimmy left a lot of his furniture at his apartment so he could rent it furnished and since I had sold or given away a lot of my furniture to avoid having to store things I no longer liked or wanted, my expenses for all this were high.

First, the decorator I hired charged me a fee up front, re-did the entire living room and family room, and then chiseled me out of about three thousand dollars that I had paid her in advance for furnishings that never arrived. She blamed the company, they blamed her, and then she eventually absconded to California, months in arrears on her local rent, so I guess we know what happened to my three thousand dollars. All this took time, aggravation, lawyers, and God-knows, and in the end I was stuck and had to replace the items that she had apparently never ordered. I changed decorators and embarked on making the smallest of the four bedrooms in the house into an office/library which worked out well, but took forever to get the carpenters to finish the built-in desk and bookshelves and then even longer to get the painters to finish painting the room. The time was getting near when I wanted to start preparation for my courses for the fall term at the college, and I couldn't even get my books and papers unpacked. I was also trying to set up another bedroom as a guest room for Christie and shopping for bedroom furniture for the master bedroom which held only a king-sized bed on a metal frame and boxes of our clothes, awaiting drawers. Everything seemed to be going to take "six to eight weeks," the repeated mantra from sellers and workers alike.

All this sounds trivial and whining now, but it was a lot of work and aggravation (and money) and I was approaching frantic every day as I kept thinking, I just want to have a home for us where we can enjoy ourselves and have friends visit. I recall at one point someone stopping in and looking into the living room which at that time was carpeted, had drapes, and had a lone table against one wall with a mirror over it. Otherwise, it was completely empty. Like what I've done with the place, I asked? I mean, we laughed, but after a while it wasn't funny.

Then there were the gardeners who, as it turned out, while probably competent in the field of lawn care, were simply not landscapers and had no clue how to design or execute what I thought was a fairly simple plan. My previous house had a lot of natural growth--woods and shrubs, and a mature collection of flower beds, already established when I moved in, so I had never required the services of a landscaper. But the new house was relatively bald, a tree line in the back, grass all over, one birch tree in front, and some base plantings along the front of the house; that was it. One side of the property was land that went uphill to the property next door and so needed bulkhead support and plantings to hold the soil. I wanted a few flower beds, some borders, some roses along a fence in a sunny spot near the garage--all of which I thought to be relatively common, simple elements of a residential property. My so-called landscaper botched almost every request with one bizarre mistake after another, the *piece de resistance* being that most of the shrubs he planted died, the five thousand dollar death we called it, because it was too late in the summer to have planted them in the first place. He never reimbursed me for anything, and I had to wait until the following spring to hire a competent landscaper and try again.

For some reason, I didn't mention any of this, the heart thing, the house and garden thing, or Jimmy getting more weird with me and still battling Christie to Dr. Waxman. I rather absorbed one after the other of the new-house issues and I suppose had gotten used to the domestic issues or hadn't related them to whatever process my counseling was involved with. I don't know. But then I got the heart palpitations worse and had the hospital visit and the pills and thought to mention my time in the hospital the next time I saw Dr. Waxman. My visits to her were not regular. Although she wanted regular, I just couldn't manage to keep to any bi-weekly schedule and so I don't recall how long it had been since I'd seen her last before my hospital adventure. I told her about it rather off-handedly, mostly interested in focusing on the eleven-minute visit from my husband and step daughter. Then she stopped me and asked a few questions and before I knew it, the whole decorator, carpenter, painter, gardener nightmare came exploding out of me in this rapid monologue ending in some anguished shout about the shrubs all dying and half my clothes still in boxes in my bedroom. I think it was maybe the look on her face that stopped me. I was never particularly demonstrative with Dr. Waxman. I never felt the need. I had a narrative. I recited it each visit. I was chronologically-based. Time, place, dates, events. And now I found myself spewing out, at a very loud pitch, all the disjointed frustrations of the last few months with little chronology or order, venting in detail for what, in retrospect, seemed like a very long time.

Silence followed and then Dr. Waxman asked me an odd question. Do you ever cry, she asked? No, I said. I hardly ever cry. You should, she responded, once a day, whether you need to or not. I thought this extremely odd at the time. Odd question, odd advice. But it shut me up. It made me for once not *think* about what I had been saying, but actually *feel* the pain of it. I don't like to feel pain. No one does. But apparently we have to, I have to. Say it. It hurts. I hurt. Cry, once a day for release rather than repression. You probably do need it.

I had many occasions over the next few years to think about that session and what it indicated about my coping skills. Later in the hour, Dr. Waxman told me: It's not that you don't cope well. It's that you cope *too* well. So what, I asked? Am I some sort of unfeeling control freak? Think about that question, was all she said. And I did; and I do. You don't have to fear losing control, she offered. No one controls much of anything. You just have to play the cards as best you can and, sometimes, no matter how well you play them, you lose. It happens. Just wait for the next deal.

So, I went home and waited for the painters, gave up on the garden until next spring, and finally got my books and papers unpacked and set up in my new office and stayed married for the next few years--until the flies came.

Part Two:
Divorce

"What God hath joined together,
let no man put asunder."

CHAPTER 8

After the glass table disaster, the cut foot, the canceled trip to Rome and my revelation in the shower, I had a divorce to plan. I decided that I would wait. Strategically, I thought it best to get past the holidays and our planned trip to St. Croix in January. Announcing my intention to divorce Jimmy prior to all these events seemed unnecessary, seemed as if it would break up all sorts of plans and disconcert too many people all at once. We normally had Thanksgiving dinner at our house and guests had already been invited. Christmas time was a busy social season in town and I had already planned our Christmas Eve open house, hiring caterers and reminding friends orally to save the date while written invitations would go out after Thanksgiving. The apartment in St. Croix had already been reserved for two weeks in January, a deposit sent, and our girls had arranged vacation time from work to go with us.

It seems odd to me now that I was putting the announcement to Jimmy of my desire for a divorce on my social calendar, booking it for late January after our return from the Caribbean, but that's what I did. It seems superficial and out of all proportion, but that's what I did. It seems cold and calculating, but that's what I did. It seems as if I was buying time to work up the courage, leave myself time to change my mind, postponing rather than acting, but that's what I did. I can only say that I shared my plan with Dr. Waxman (and no one else) and she didn't faint or chastise me, so that's what I did. I planned and I prayed and I got along, each day, by telling myself that I would soon have peace. It was my mantra. Peace. Love, companionship, a partner with whom to share life--these would all be gone but in their place, peace. After years of strain and effort and war, I wanted peace. Doesn't every war-weary person, people, nation feel the same? I think so.

The thing was, I loved Jimmy. He was beautiful and, when sane, very funny, smart, conversant, pleasant to be with and, if not exactly exciting, as promised, seldom totally boring. I was sexually drawn to him and he was a good lover, generous, gentle and passionate. I also felt deeply moved by his dysfunction that I was still not calling an illness. I just somehow concluded that his definition of marriage was not my definition. That his cruelty, however motivated, was unbearable for me and irreparable. I believed and still believe that I had tried everything I knew how to try. My choice was to grin and bear it, aware that Jimmy was not wholly aware of the pain he caused me, or end it. I chose the latter; it seemed inevitable.

I knew telling Jimmy that I wanted a divorce would not necessarily come as a great surprise to him in the conventional sense. He had to know, after all, that our life together was one of constant and unpleasant disruption. But I knew that, regardless, he did not handle rejection well. In many ways, his life had been a series of rejections--by wives, children, employers, colleagues, and acquaintances who thought him rude or arrogant, which he surely could be. And I knew that on a couple of occasions, he had had serious emotional problems following major rejections in his life. I had to try to factor this into my thinking as I knew there would be a period of time, after I broke the news, that we would still have to live together and that, somehow, during that time, until he left, we'd both have to survive each other. I am talking about emotional rather than physical survival--and I knew that if we were suffering now, that suffering would only get worse unless we could figure out a way, hopefully together, to manage.

I talked about this with Dr. Waxman who seemed to imply that since I could not do anything about what he would do and would probably have limited ability to provide help for Jimmy, I would have to strengthen my own coping strategies. I could not be his soon-to-be-ex wife and his therapist at the same time. I mean, I knew that perception was all, that the way I viewed the experience would *be* the experience, but that was often easier to say than to live. I think I just kept filing these thoughts away, however. I think I believed that it would be such a relief to finally begin to end the marriage that this relief would be enough to see me through. I was wrong, but that's what I thought.

Somehow we got through the holidays with a reasonably festive Thanksgiving gathering, lots of helter-skelter and a few daiquiris in the kitchen, some pleasant holiday parties, my own Christmas eve open house, and a nice New Year's Eve spent dining with a few couples of Jimmy's acquaintance. The good thing about all this busy-ness, plus the end-of-semester grading and wrapping up my courses, was that it made time speed by and served as a welcome distraction from my other agenda. I did, from time to time, think, oh, what the hell; why not struggle on, take the good with the bad, just stay married and absorb the trauma. But these thoughts didn't stay. Staying was no longer possible. I loved and liked Jimmy, but was miserable being married to him. That was just the incontrovertible truth that I could never walk away from. Like so many others before me, I had thought marriage would ease the frictions in the dating relationship. Unfortunately, like so many others, I found marriage only made the frictions worse. I never really blamed Jimmy, *per se*; I focused more on the fact that I just couldn't live this way, that I had tried everything I knew how to try. I asked Jimmy several times if he'd be willing to go for marriage counseling with me and he said that the only thing wrong with our marriage was me and so, no, he wouldn't go for marriage counseling. Maybe he was right. Maybe I was to blame and should have continued to play the dating game or remained the princess in the tower. The point was, I no longer cared whose fault it was. Never really one for the blame game, I learned that placing blame solves little. Figuring out how to solve the problem was more my *modus operandi* and then I just ran out of options: On to the final solution.

So after that black night in St. Croix, with Jimmy still crazily dreaming dreams of purchasing land and building a house on the island, we made our way home. I spent a few quiet days getting the cat from the kennel, unpacking and washing, straightening up, doing domestic things. Then, on the third night after we got back, I cooked a nice dinner and while we had our coffee afterward, told Jimmy I wanted a divorce. I said something like since it appeared that we were both miserable much of the time, and I had run out of tricks, I thought it might be best to call it quits. Never one to be caught with his guard down, Jimmy told me he was ten times more miserable than I could ever be and, had I not mentioned divorce, he certainly would have. As he said this, I could see the wounded expression on his face in stark contrast to his words, but I let him rant on. He reiterated that the only thing wrong with our marriage was me, queen bee, bitch, whatever. I told him that he was probably right but felt that it might be more productive to talk about arrangements. I asked that he move out of the house as soon as possible, not later than a month (which seemed like an eternity to me), that he take everything that was his (since our rejection of joint property would make that pretty clear), and that we let our lawyers talk about what should be a fairly simple legal parting--short-term marriage, no children, no property issues, no custody issues, no joint holdings of any sort, no alimony. Clean and neat. I thought.

I don't recall any further reaction from Jimmy that evening, except that he said, under the circumstances, he thought it best that I move out of the bedroom. I was about to say that I thought that was my line and since it was my house, my bed, and my bedroom furniture, I didn't think this sounded *best* at all; but I didn't say any of that (no queen bee there!) and just immediately began moving a supply of clothes and personal items into Bella's room, which wasn't really fully Bella's room anymore, except for when she came home, as she lived and worked in another state by now. I could have chosen the guest room to move into and perhaps should have, but somehow I felt more comforted being surrounded by Bella's things, her aura still very much present in the room, even though she occupied it only sporadically. I had also put my old cat's litter box and food in there for him. The cat liked that room best in the house, perhaps because he missed Bella, and at twenty-one years old, he didn't get around too well, and so I gave him the room he preferred in which to spend his golden years. So, I de-camped from my bedroom to share space with my lovely old cat, Pussy, who only ever just slept and ate, the two of us embraced within the spell of Bella. Upon consideration, I counted this as a very good deal.

I do remember very clearly, however, what Jimmy chose to do in the ensuing weeks. He communicated minimally or not at all. He slept or pretended to sleep until I left for work, was not home when I got back from work, and came home very late most nights. Bella's room was situated over the garage that housed Jimmy's car and so he would wake me every night when he got home at one or two AM by using the garage door opener which vibrated loudly in Bella's room, making me leap out of a deep sleep at the vibrant noise and with terror for the first week or so that this went on. He went out both weekend days as well, all day, and did the late night arrivals then, too. My sleep was being seriously impaired by all this, but then I suppose that was the idea. I also developed a serious case of chronic heartburn that made it difficult to eat and even more difficult to sleep, as I continued to anticipate the sounds of the garage door, and I lost ten pounds as a result. I think I was looking rather forlorn and my friends began to worry about me.

One night when Jimmy got home about eight PM, instead of his usual wee-hour arrival, I asked if he was making any progress in finding a place to live. It was more than a month since I had asked him to leave and I didn't know how much longer I could go on with such tension on such little sleep--although I never mentioned the lack of sleep, just saying that I'd like to get things moving. He started yelling almost immediately that his apartment wouldn't be free until July first and did I know how hard it was to get a short-term furnished rental. I agreed and said I believed it might, in fact, be difficult to re-locate for these few months, but said I couldn't have him in the house until July. He responded by saying that if I were willing to share the moving costs with him, he thought he might be able to work things out. He said that since it was my fault that he'd have to move twice, this was only fair and I guessed this made a certain amount of sense. I asked him how much and when he told me, a thousand dollars (a pretty steep moving cost, I thought), I immediately wrote him a check for the amount. He accepted it by saying, see, you can have anything you want if you're willing to pay for it, a line from a bad movie, I thought. Unaccountably, this transaction seemed to infuriate him and he suddenly reached for the telephone, the object closest at hand, and threw it at me. Those were the days when telephones were attached to the wall outlet by a cord and so the phone he threw didn't go more than a few feet and didn't come anywhere near me.

Nonetheless, I calmly picked up my purse, got a coat and left without a word. I drove over to the house of friends, rather surprised them with my unannounced visit, and said I just needed a place to sit for a few hours. They gave me a brandy, let me sit, and best of all, did not ask me anything--except if I wanted to spend the night. I said no, I thought things would be OK within a few hours and, indeed, when I got home a little after ten, Jimmy was apparently asleep and I got my first full-night's sleep in a month with no garage-door interval. I did lock the door to Bella's room, however, something I hadn't felt the need to do before.

The next day, a Thursday, Jimmy was again home early that evening and announced he'd be moving out the following Monday, and when I got home from work that following Monday evening, purposely quite a bit later than usual, he was indeed gone, leaving no forwarding address or information. He had done no advance packing or loading of his car that I was aware of, but when I got home that Monday night, he was gone without a trace, like magic, like Gretchen. He had taken all his things, everything, and some wedding gifts given to us by his friends, plus he took the two main TVs in the house (one of which was mine) leaving only a small, old TV I had in the kitchen. Oddly, he left me two lovely wing-backed Kittinger chairs that were his, but that I had had re-upholstered for the big living room makeover in a fabric that he chose to hate upon sight. I guess the message was that I had ruined his chairs so might as well keep them.

I made myself a strong martini and sat in one of those chairs in a small state of shock as I assessed the damage.

The entire dining room was vacant, the furniture belonging to Jimmy. The kitchen table remained but the chairs (his) were gone. A side table in the foyer and some lamps and decorative items were gone. Other than the TV, I couldn't see from my vantage point that he had taken anything that didn't belong to him, but it was still a shock to see the house so strangely stripped, to see what had been our home that morning turned into this freaky half-furnished dwelling so quickly, indentation marks from the gone furniture all over the carpets. I don't think I had quite believed him when he said he'd be out on Monday, but now he was and it seemed so sudden, so silent, and so empty in a disjointed way. Here today; gone today.

I just sat and sipped my drink over the next half hour, and I slowly began to feel a transformation. A word was struggling to make its way to the surface of my mind and it finally took shape and had meaning. Peace. Peace. Peace.

CHAPTER 9

Bella was wonderful in those first weeks after Jimmy moved out. She came home every weekend and not only helped me shop for replacement items and furnishings--something about which I felt an obsessive urgency--but she also provided quiet love and companionship, a morale boost, and the sense that things were now righted again, that the topsy-turvy existence of the past five years had not been the norm but that this, this here-and-now present, was the re-establishment of some sort of cosmic balance. She grounded me.

One Saturday when we were shopping at a popular electronic store called Crazy Eddie's to replace the television from the family room (I had decided to hang on to the old but serviceable kitchen TV), the unimaginable happened: Jimmy walked into the store. Of all the electronic stores in the county, he had to pick this one, isn't that how it goes? I started to panic, but cool as could be, Bella walked up to him while I hid out in one of the aisles and asked him if he'd mind leaving until we had finished shopping. You're upsetting my mother, she said, very simply, and unbelievably, Jimmy acquiesced and left. Sure, he said; you be a good girl, Bella. Ever the 50's dad.

One Friday night Bella and I were at the Pier, a local waterfront bar and restaurant, having a late supper, when Gretchen and George came in and spotted us. I hadn't seen either of them in a few years. I pushed aside my unfinished steamers and grabbed my glass of wine for fortification as they came up to our table, Gretchen looking very glamorous in a tight strapless black sequined top and bleached-out jeans, George looking drunk. They made a tremendous deal out of congratulating me on my soon-to-be divorce, saying in too-loud voices how I should have gotten rid of the bum long ago or never married him in the first place. Since I knew many of the people at the bar and at various tables throughout the restaurant, in one way or another, I was feeling terribly exposed and embarrassed by their sudden show of high-volume support for me when, after all, they--or, at least George-- were supposedly Jimmy's friends and thus presumed to be in Jimmy's camp (those his-or-her camps that are established after couples separate). For whatever reason, they were now my new best friends, dissing Jimmy on multiple counts and almost sanctifying my forbearance. I thanked them, refused their offer of a drink saying that we were about to leave, and eventually they left our table, taking a distant seat at the bar. Well, that was weird, Bella said after they left. Especially, I added, when you consider that I helped Gretchen pack when she moved out on George several years ago! Apparently they had since gotten married and bought a huge home in Florida where they spent much of their time, returning to a local condo only sporadically. Ain't love grand. Bella and I paid up and left, giving Gretchen and George a huge wave as we walked out. They yoo-hooed us back. Your fans, Bella muttered.

Other friends were also supportive. They called, invited me to dinner or to parties, didn't pry, fixed me up with men on occasion, and provided a foundation on which I felt I might be able to build a good, if diminished, new life. An acquaintance named Lee who lived very close to me became more friendly post-Jimmy--frequently inviting me over last-minute to join her and her husband for dinner, convenient because I could walk the two streets over to her house in five minutes. It was thoughtful of her and casual enough that I didn't feel like a burden. I call you when I have too much food for two, she'd say. Perfect. While we waited for dinner to cook, Lee and I would sit on her back porch, overlooking a back yard dominated by a pool, drinking wine and pleasantly talking about everything. We talked about the fact that her husband had just received a promotion at work that would involve more traveling and time away from home, something about which she felt ambivalent. She was pleased with the promotion, but frightened in a lot of ways about the increased time apart it would involve. We talked about friends we had in common, about her children and grandchildren, about local politics, and about my divorce. My divorce.

I had engaged my regular lawyer, Gabe, and said I'd let him know when I heard who Jimmy's lawyer would be. He drew up some paper work for a legal separation until the divorce could be processed. After six weeks, having heard precisely nothing from the party of the second part, I gave my lawyer Jimmy's work number since I had no idea where Jimmy was living. Not long after that, I had a surprise visit from Jimmy. It was a sunny Saturday morning in March, brighter and warmer than it should have been for that time of year. It heralded spring which was making me feel cheerful. Thank God Bella was there for the weekend, because when I answered the ring of the doorbell and saw Jimmy standing there, my heart started doing its somersault thing. He was dressed in a dark blue suit, white shirt, bright yellow paisley tie and had on his dramatic face. Long, long time since I crossed this threshold, he said to Bella who stood behind me in the foyer with her mouth open. For Christ's sake, Jimmy, I said, it's been five weeks and then I just turned and walked back into the kitchen where I had been sitting with Bella when the doorbell rang.

He eventually followed Bella into the kitchen noticing, I hoped, the nice new kitchen chairs, and continued his dramatic monologue: Many miles have been traveled, good things have happened, bad things are all behind me. Assuming that I was one of the bad things that were behind him, I didn't answer. He went on to tell us about various private business ventures he was launching, one more nuts than the other. The one I remember most was how he was starting a senior women's golfing tour for TV and had flown down to Texas to engage the support of Patty Berg. Always short on the practical details, he never mentioned how he hoped to accomplish this, how the LPGA felt about his little plan, how Patty Berg at 70-something was going to manage playing golf competitively, and how he would manage TV coverage and sponsorships since the regular women's tour was barely able to get coverage on cable TV. He also had some notion about a Canadian Freedom Train where he was going to take a famous black American singer from America to Canada and have her ride the freedom train back to the USA along with hundreds of black Canadians all singing something like God Bless America. At this point, I stopped listening. I was frightened. He was just inches short of raving, albeit he spoke in a low, modulated cadence, like the narrator of a documentary on PBS.

The next thing I knew, he and Bella were going outside to see his alleged new car, and as I looked out the window, I saw Bella actually get into the car with him and watched them both drive away before I could really register what was happening. I panicked. The first thing I thought of was to call the police--I'm a great believer in 911--but I couldn't figure out what to tell them. Bella seemed to have gotten into the car willingly. It was another new white Cadillac, but I didn't know what model and had no clue as to the license plate number. What would I tell the police? That my 25-year old baby had been kidnapped by my soon-to-be-ex-husband? I paced around, lit a cigarette and decided I'd call the police, regardless, if they didn't get back by the time I'd smoked it. Just as I was stubbing out the cigarette, the white Cadillac pulled back into the driveway, Bella got out, and I started to breathe again. She came into the house as Jimmy drove away and said he's totally nuts. Then why did you go with him, I almost screamed, as Bella poured herself the last of the morning coffee. Because he's harmless, she said. Just, you know, delusional. Still, I said. Don't do that again. Crazy is crazy; you never know. Oh, he just wanted to show off to us, she said, you know, about how well he's doing, doesn't need us, big tycoon, all that macho crap. I thought it was probably a good idea to let him, Bella continued, you know, to be impressed like he wanted, maybe save you some grief later on. Grief, I said, would have been if he'd kidnapped you, possibly to put you on the Canadian Freedom Train or the women's golf tour or something. And with that, we both began to laugh hysterically. Poor, poor Jimmy, I said, when we calmed down, suddenly feeling very sad about him.

Not long after that, I had a call from one of Jimmy's best friends, John, who had been very kind to me giving good advice and help with replacing electronics after the break-up and who now asked me, with clear concern in his voice, if I thought it was possible that Jimmy might be drinking to excess. No, I said, too much alcohol makes him sick; but he's crazy. I told John about the senior women's golf, Patty Berg, the Freedom Train, and the rest of his visit to us, with all its delusional details. Apparently Jimmy had been guilty of some pretty bizarre public behaviors within the past few months that John and some of Jimmy's other friends were trying to understand or explain by excessive drinking, but I told John that I thought not, or that, at least, he had not been drinking the morning that he visited my house and absconded briefly with Bella. I think it's all part of his inability to cope with our separation, I explained further, even though he'd never cop to that; and, perhaps it's symptomatic of an intensification of whatever psychological problem he has, a problem, I told John, that I was now beginning to think was clinical. I mean, I added, he is clearly borderline delusional and that strikes me as very serious.

John went on to tell me, apparently believing after what I said that I was ready to hear it, that it appeared that Jimmy was about to get married to a French Canadian woman he had been dating, commuting to Canada to do so, that he had been inviting all his friends to attend the wedding to be held in Montreal, date TBA. Well, I said, it might be nice if he divorced me first to, you know, avoid any bigamy complications. John had long ago given up any notions that Jimmy could ever be expected to act for long in line with any social conventions whatsoever, but I think the idea that Jimmy was psychotic had not fully occurred to him and perhaps was just now beginning to sink in as a real possibility. It was strange that this possibility occurred to no one over Jimmy's long and complicated history. Stranger still was the fact that it had not occurred to me until lately, nor to his best friend John until today. John and I were both intelligent people, had enjoyed long complex political conversations, enlivening dinners at the club; we respected each other's minds, and yet neither of us had for one second conceived this truth about Jimmy or anything close to it. It seems incredulous and yet so it was. We talked for a little longer. John seemed to be working over what I had said and eventually suggested that perhaps he could get Jimmy to seek some kind of help, stopping short of saying see a psychiatrist. I don't know, I said. I didn't have much success along those lines but, perhaps, coming from you, it might stick, especially if he is as frantic as he seems. I mean, he's making up a whole new fantasy life as he goes along; when does reality come crashing in and what happens when it does?

What happened when reality did hit the fan of his delusions was more horrific than any of us could have imagined. But I was not imagining the ending at this point. I was just sitting on Lee's back porch, drinking wine, telling her about Jimmy's visit, John's call, and the new chick in Jimmy's delusional life. Lee was of the opinion that separated meant just that: separate, separate lives. She was of the further opinion that I was still being pulled into Jimmy's orbit, still thrashing around with his issues as if I had a stake in them which, she said, I should *not* have. Your only issue is the divorce and you're paying your lawyer for that. I tried to avoid hearing and responding to what she was saying, but I knew it was true. She asked me if I still loved him and I just laughed and said that was hardly the point. But I guess I feel guilty, I said. I mean, if he got cancer and I dumped him, I'd be horribly cruel. But he got mentally ill and I dumped him, so what does that say about me? You didn't know, Lee said. And he didn't "just get" mentally ill. Obviously, this has been going on for a long time, long before you met him, and while you sensed something, you didn't know. You still don't, really. So, there's a huge difference between leaving someone who discovers he is physically ill and ending a marriage gone haywire for whatever reasons. Just be glad you're out of it and *be* out of it.

I agreed with Lee; I really did. I told myself that no matter what my feelings for or about Jimmy might be, he and I just had no place else to go. We had exhausted every relationship avenue. I had some vague notion that we might remain friends in some indefinite and misty future, when everything that had gone on between us was well into the past. I never let this thought take any more definite shape than maybe, some day; but then I've always hated goodbyes, even when they were desirable.

Less than two weeks after my conversation with Lee about how separation means separate, Jimmy called. He sounded very normal on the phone. He asked that I meet him for dinner to discuss the details of our divorce, sounding rather pleasantly professional as if we might be going to talk about the sale of a house or a pending securities purchase. Without giving it too much thought (he had the advantage of surprise as I was definitely not expecting either the call or a mention of the divorce), I agreed to meet him the following night at a restaurant about half way between my house and his apartment--the apartment he owned but was not yet back living in. I actually still didn't know where he was living.

Following the phone conversation, I had a little conversation in my head with an imaginary Lee, explaining to her that since neither my lawyer nor I had heard much from Jimmy about the divorce proceedings, I really did want to talk about this face-to-face in the hopes of moving things along. I mean, it's not as if it's a date or something that won't have to happen some time or other, no matter where, so I think I should go to try to avoid further delay. In my mind, I almost had Lee convinced until I heard her reply: Tell him to talk to your lawyer. And I knew that this was exactly what I should have said. Foiled again, as they say.

But I felt strangely unperturbed as I drove to the restaurant to meet Jimmy the next night. I had no demands to make, no recriminations to express, no complaints whatsoever in mind. Since our separation, I had no further desire to discuss what had gone wrong or whether or not the marriage could be saved or what he owed me or anything along those lines. So I could not imagine that this dinner meeting would produce a confrontational conversation. To the contrary, I had in mind that if there really was a French Canadian fiancée in the picture, then Jimmy would have every reason to want to move our divorce along, file the papers, get the decree, and have that wedding in Montreal. I just assumed this new affair had been his motivation and, crazy or not, he certainly had to realize that he could not marry anyone (legally) until he unmarried me. My lawyer had originally indicated that the entire process would probably take about six months, barring any complications, and so I guessed that Jimmy wanted to get things going. Keep in mind, Jimmy needed a certain kind of woman to marry. While he was relatively self-sufficient financially after surviving several set-backs and would not marry for money, he did need to marry someone who was relatively financially self sufficient, since his finances would not extend to supporting a second person in the style in which he wanted to live. He could buy himself a Cadillac; his wife would have to buy her own. In addition, the woman would have to have some sort of education and some sort of mind and wit. Jimmy might be crazy, but he was neither stupid nor dull. He also appreciated style; and she would, of course, have to be thin and blond as all his wives had been. I'm sure he would have also preferred someone under fifty--or at least someone who *looked* to be under fifty. In short, the woman that Jimmy needed for wife number four was not

one too readily available. Had he found one, I would guess
he would want to hang on to her and seal the deal, although
why he wanted to marry again was beyond me since he was
obviously so unsuited for it. On the other hand, he was
infinitely needy. Not my problem, I was thinking, as I pulled
into the restaurant parking lot, prepared to make it as easy
as possible for Jimmy to take the plunge once again.

He was already there when I arrived, seated and waiting
to order drinks until I arrived. He ordered his usual vodka
on the rocks with a twist and I ordered a Manhattan. The
restaurant was one we had visited a few times in the past,
a sort of landmark place in the county, same ownership
for years, little change in decor, a menu that had a heavy
emphasis on steaks, chops and seafood. It was paneled in
dark wood with low lights lending luster to the wood's
finish, rather like a posh men's club. The carpet was thick,
the tablecloths sparkling white, a very nice traditional place
and the kind in which Jimmy was most comfortable. Fine
with me. He looked attractive, perhaps a little too thin, but
dressed in his blue blazer, grey flannels, pale blue oxford
shirt, and another nicely patterned yellow tie. I noticed that
his hair looked a little thinner with a little blond tint and I
was about to ask him whether he was dying his hair, until
I thought better of it. He asked after Bella while we waited
for our drinks and I brought him up to date on her job and
a little personal stuff, dating a nice man called Randy, I told
him, for a few months now. When the drinks arrived and
we took our first sips in silence, Jimmy turned his attention
to the menu, although I could have told him what he would
order before he even opened it, and he did. He picked a New

York strip steak, medium rare, and I selected soft shell crab. We closed our menus and while we waited for the waiter's return to take our orders, no rush Jimmy had told him, he said rather abruptly that he was going to represent himself in the divorce, didn't need to pay a goddamned lawyer, and that I should just have my lawyer file the divorce complaint and then serve him with the papers after the filing. He thought that a no-fault, irreconcilable differences divorce would be the fastest. He said he'd review the filing, and, if all things were in order, no complications, he'd sign and return it. I nodded my total agreement, told him what documents my lawyer needed from him, gave him a typed list with my lawyer's address, and asked, perfectly straight-faced, where my lawyer should send the paperwork. He hesitated for just a moment and then said rather quickly that he should just send them on to his office, registered. He handed me a business card (in case I had forgotten where his office was?). Absolutely, I said. Perfect. I'll call Gabe tomorrow.

And that was our discussion about the divorce., all three minutes of it. Not another word. He had dictated, I had quit while I was ahead, and we spent the rest of the evening in small talk about sports, current events, and, if you exclude a rather flamboyant soliloquy apropos of nothing that he inserted into the conversation, raving about Gabrielle, the French Canadian, it was a perfectly ordinary evening. In fact, even the little distraction about the fiancée didn't unbalance me. I was actually indebted to her for this quickie-divorce, no animosity man at my table and so I just listened as he extolled her virtues, her beauty, the elegance of her Montreal apartment, and I managed again to keep my face under full control as I congratulated him on finding such a lovely woman and wished him the best of everything. I had no idea whether or not she was real or was as he described her and found that I didn't care. I didn't care at all. After we finished our entree and our wine, shared a crème brulee for desert, and split the bill--which surprised the waiter a bit since he had us pegged as a totally different kind of couple--Jimmy walked me out to my car and bid me good night.

His demeanor during the entire evening was perfect, far too perfect. He was like a man playing a part which, of course, was exactly what he was, an actor in another role, high drama from his perspective. When I drove home, I had to blink to keep the tears inside my eyes as I was more convinced than ever that he was even more out of touch with reality than before, that he was now not dad from Father Knows Best, but some suave dilettante from a Noel Coward play, getting rid of the old lady in order to embark on a brand new exciting journey in life and love, running golf tournaments and the Freedom Train in his spare time. It was the most tragic dinner date I had ever had.

CHAPTER 10

Not wanting to let Jimmy's new commitment to our severance cool, I contacted my lawyer the next morning and told him to get things going, to file the complaint and then serve Jimmy as soon as the court registered the filing. No frills, I told him; keep it as simple as the law allows. No fault, no relief, no property distribution. He took some further information from me over the phone, told me what additional documents he would need me to send in addition to those already requested of Jimmy, and said he thought he could get the papers ready for filing in a month, maybe sooner. After he had the court's acknowledgement, he could then serve Jimmy via his lawyer and then we'd wait for a court date. When I told him that Jimmy was doing this *pro se*, he sounded a little displeased--a lawyer thing, I guess--but I didn't inquire further, just hoped silently that this wouldn't add complications and let it go.

My lawyer had also told me to send him a final list of events going back at least six months or more that would demonstrate "irreconcilable differences" and the nature of this request disturbed me. I wanted to be hands off in this, didn't want to engage in further battle. I tried to think of how to write the specifics that would be persuasive but not caustic. I would have to write this very carefully, sharing blame, creating a scenario that would not push Jimmy into defensive mode. I pondered whether or not Gabrielle should go on the list. Surely a fiancée qualified as an irreconcilable difference?

Early that evening, just as I got home from work, I had a call from Lee. She was bummed out. Her husband had to be out of town on business for three days, her daughter was having romance problems, long story she said, and she'd just had to leave her dog with the veterinarian due to some mysterious dog illness that the vet wanted to "observe." Sounds like you need some TLC, I said. Why don't you come over here, I suggested, and we'll get a pizza or something. But Lee wanted to go out for drinks and dinner, emphasis on the drinks, she said. So we arranged to meet at the club at seven. I had just been out the night before and was sort of looking forward to a night at home, bath, early to bed. But she had been so kind to me over the past weeks that I felt I owed her a night out.

A little after seven, we were settled at the bar with our cocktails. I was expecting to be a sympathetic ear for her, listening to her issues about the husband's new responsibilities or the daughter's love issues, when she surprised me and asked if I felt uncomfortable. Uncomfortable, I asked, not sure to what part of my damaged little life she was referring. I mean, you know, she said, being here with everyone in the club talking about your divorce and then Jimmy dating Mavis. Heavens, I said. That was a mouthful. I don't care what everyone's saying, if that's what you mean by uncomfortable, because there's nothing too exciting to be saying. And I didn't know Jimmy was dating Mavis. I mean, isn't Mavis still married to Everett? Well, Lee amended, let's just say that Jimmy was seen with Mavis at the Jolly Oyster, apparently having dinner--and, no, Mavis and Everett separated about a month ago, so I guess they are not staying married. With that, I had to tell her about my dinner with Jimmy the night before and about the lovely Gabrielle. I hesitated to do this because as much as I liked Lee, I knew she wasn't gossip-proof and since I wasn't sure whether or not Gabrielle was even real, I had been intending to keep her to myself for the time being. But I was confused about Jimmy being out with Mavis and felt compelled to counter this news. I was also a little hurt that Jimmy would choose to take out someone from my town, actually a casual friend with whom I played golf and exchanged chatter from time to time. Mavis, I said again; what the hell would she want to go out with Jimmy for? He's got to be twenty plus years older than she is. And he's nuts. I know, said Lee. Just saying, you should know. Yeah, I said. OK. I'm glad you told me. Now how about the husband, the daughter, and the dog? And we did finally spent the rest of the night on Lee's stories and not mine.

A few days later, oddly enough, I had a call from Mavis. She was brief, said she wanted to talk to me about something, could we meet somewhere for dinner? I had a strong idea of what she wanted to talk to me about and I wasn't sure I wanted that conversation, but curiosity got the better of me and so I agreed to meet her at a new little restaurant out of town. I hadn't seen Mavis for a while and so when I met her the following week, as arranged, I was impressed all over again by what a beautiful woman she was. You tend to get inured to the beauty of your friends but then get reminded of it all over again when you haven't seen them for a while. She was incredibly tiny, perfect in every detail, had one of those thin sculptured faces that you know will just never really age. She had blond hair of indeterminate length, sort of chopped long and short, and very blue eyes staring out from under a straight brow. She made me feel big and clumsy even though I really wasn't. Hey, I said, as I sat down at the table determined to be cheery, how's everything? Well, she said, don't even ask because I might tell you. And then she did. It seems that Everett, her husband of about five years, a second marriage for both, was having some sort of horrible breakdown, living more or less in their basement, barely communicating with her in any way. She told me so much about this breakdown and all the attendant weird behavior, through drinks and salad and into the main course, that I wondered if perhaps I had been mistaken, that she hadn't asked to meet to talk about "dating Jimmy" at all, as I had naturally supposed.

But then we got to that. She was almost apologetic, even though I told her there was no need since Jimmy and I were totally over, done. She said he'd been after her for weeks, phoning and then stopping by after Everett moved out, and had kind of trapped her into dinner at the Jolly Oyster, turning a meet after work for a drink into an entire evening. The point was, she had no interest. She didn't particularly care for him, felt he was too old for her, and on and on with *sorry* punctuating all these revelations. Don't be sorry, I said. He's twenty-five years older than you, far too old, and you don't have to like him just because I married him.

I also thought that part of Jimmy's pursuit of her was to try to stick it to me, embarrass me on my own turf, but I never said this. I let her vent for a little while longer and then told her that her business was with Jimmy and not with me. She was free to see him or not (not, she interjected) without even a thought about my interests, because I had none. I added, however, that he was a persistent man and so she had better be very clear, very soon if she wanted to be rid of him.

She seemed then to relax and returned to the story of her own marital breakdown and her feelings, similar to mine about my own marriage, that she and Everett were over. We spent the rest of the dinner, through desert and coffee, in a kind of divorce sisterhood, laughing a lot, and, oddly, bonding. Before we left she asked that I not repeat a word of what she told me. I didn't extract the same promise from her, I didn't care, but I told her I wouldn't say anything about the details of her and Everett's break, and I never did. I never even told her about Gabrielle. Somehow, it seemed strangely irrelevant. But I think Mavis and I both left the restaurant feeling better about whatever things in this situation had troubled us and in an odd way felt more comforted, less alone. As it turned out, Mavis never saw Jimmy again and Gabrielle eventually became a major drama. But that came later.

CHAPTER 11

So, I mean, that's the thing about divorce. No matter how you want the peace of the ending as soon as possible, it's just never simple. Tell me about a simple divorce and I'll tell you someone's probably lying.

I dragged myself through March and the dull dog end of winter. I had taken on an extra course to teach for the spring term, late afternoons on Tuesdays and Thursdays, because I wanted to be busier. I rarely took overload courses because my schedule was full enough, teaching three classes and serving as coordinator of the English program at the college. But I thought the extra course would take more time away from unoccupied time, time when I would worry about the divorce. I had found that while at school, teaching or doing curricular and administrative work, I barely thought about my marriage at all. I had always been able to compartmentalize and I think that was very helpful for me.

My late afternoon overload class, however, had turned into a minor disaster. It was the lowest level remedial writing course and, given the hour it was offered (3:30 to 5:00PM), it attracted only the most desperate or rejected of students, those Charlie-come-lately wanderers who took courses that were still open or that some counselor had told them they needed. It had started out as a small enough section, about fifteen students, and was already reduced to about ten. I saw every form of need in the students in this class. One boy was so learning disabled that he was able to produce only one sentence in the original writing sample (given 45 minutes to complete), a sentence that was actually a sentence fragment. He was a bright boy and reasonably articulate orally, but had the kind of paralysis with writing that I hardly knew how to approach. I had no training in teaching the learning disabled and had to try anything that I was able to pick up from reading about the handicapped learner. I never knew what would work. There was a girl in the class who sat front-row, center, and stared at me intensely, always with a slight frown through very thick glasses. She had a colorful three-ring binder, magic marker pens tucked into a brightly colored plastic pen holder, looking as if she were ready for third grade. I estimated her IQ to be about 80, her essays of the see-Spot-run variety--all simple sentences, no ideas, the sentences not even vaguely related to the essay topic or, on most occasions, to each other. There was another boy who turned out to be fifteen years old. After about two weeks in the class, he told me he had quit high school last October as a sophomore and now wanted to try college. I was able to get this young man removed from the course, but, sadly, he did not understand, thought me a major ogre. He had been functionally illiterate as well as being fifteen years old with one year of high school to his credit and a very unsuccessful year at that. Most of the remaining students had serious problems--with language, with logic, and, from the look of them, with finances, nutrition, and basic social skills. It was just the saddest group of students I had ever had. I thought only one or two had enough of the basic fundaments of literacy to have a chance of passing the course. It created for me one of those moments in the career of a community college professor when one wondered what it was all about. As this was a low period in my own life, I think I felt greater despair about this class than I might normally have felt. As a result, I expended a great deal of energy on each of the remaining ten students and felt every instance of their failure to prosper as a personal failure.

One Thursday evening, in early April, after spending about an hour after this class ended tutoring the severely dyslexic boy, I got home about 6:30 to a message on my answering machine from my lawyer, Gabe. He said to call him at home whenever I got this message and so I did. He truly was my friend as well as my lawyer. We talked for a bit and then he told me that he had filed my divorce papers and sent Jimmy copies of the filing. Jimmy had called him and said he couldn't sign right away because he was considering seeking relief in the form of alimony. Since we had already verbally agreed that there would be no strings in the filing, no form of relief sought, I was at first shocked by this, then angered, and then very suddenly dispirited. Can he do that, I asked? Well, of course, he can do anything, Gabe replied, but he'll never get alimony. Hell, he said, *you* couldn't get alimony under the circumstances. This is shit, I said, excuse my language. He's just trying to be annoying. What do you want to do, he asked. Offer him a cash incentive, I said, something apart from the divorce, just a little money gift, to help further cover his relocation costs. My lawyer did not think this petty bribery was wise, so I said, OK, let this play out, see where he goes with it and for how long, but if you think he would take a little cash bonus at some point, make the offer--maybe hypothetically and, of course, not in writing. He agreed and this was where we left it.

Before the call I had been quite hungry, but after it my appetite vanished. I had been having stomach problems on and off throughout the past months, horrible attacks of heartburn continued even after the mid night garage door assaults, no matter what I ate. I saw the doctor about it and at first he wanted to do all sorts of tests but when I told him I was going through a divorce, he said, oh, right, and wrote me a prescription. I took one of the pills he had prescribed and just sat there looking at my uneaten food, trying to be calm, hoping my stomach would settle and my appetite would return. I really was unattractively thin (yes, you *can* be too thin) and didn't want to miss yet another meal. Just then, the phone rang again and I considered not answering it. But I picked up and it was Bella, just calling to see how I was doing. I didn't want to burden her with this latest set back, but she could tell from my voice that something was up so I mentioned Jimmy's little request for time in order to consider alimony. She was livid, angry enough for both of us, and said she was going to call him and tell him what a crazy bastard he was. No, I said, please. Maybe later, but not now. Let Gabe handle it right now. So Bella said she would come down for the weekend, maybe Saturday morning. Oh, honey, I said, that would be wonderful. And it was.

I spent Friday night and most of Saturday morning doing school work so that I would be free to spend all my time with Bella over the weekend. We went out for lunch shortly after she arrived and I found that I was really hungry and was able to eat without debilitating heartburn. You're better than those pills the doctor gave me, I told her. We pigged out on California burgers, fries, and huge diet cokes. After we ate, looking out the restaurant windows at the river which marked the southern border of our county, little boats bobbing along in the wake of large cruisers, we talked about Jimmy and the vagaries of our life together, about how he was probably having a hard time letting go. That's what Christie thinks, Bella said. You know, I said, I haven't talked to her in weeks. Maybe I should call her. She called me last week, Bella said. She was really upset about Jimmy and this new chick, the French Canada woman, whatever. Has Christie met her, I asked Bella? Well, apparently no one has actually met her, Bella said, but Jimmy is allegedly spending a fortune flying up to Montreal to see her, and from what he told Christie, he bought her a $20,000 diamond ring for the engagement. No wonder he wants alimony, I said cynically.

Bella asked me why I didn't consider asking *him* for alimony as a counter-measure. Well, I said, first of all, I don't want any alimony from him so it would be a dishonest request. I don't want to play games and I don't want to prolong this thing with needless complications. There really are no issues in dispute and I don't see why he wants to create them just to drag the thing out. I just want him gone, you know. Bella agreed, but then said, you know how he can get. Oh yes, I said. I know.

After lunch, we went home and sat down at the kitchen table to talk a little. I turned on the little kitchen TV so we could watch the golf while we chatted and the TV didn't come on. I checked the plug and the cable box connections, but they were all in place. On a hunch, Bella went out onto the deck off the kitchen and found the cable wire, cut neatly in half. I just looked at her and we both knew what we were thinking. Call the police, she said. What for, I shrugged despondently. This could have been done by anyone, they'll never be able to find out. Yeah, Bella said, but it's just good to have it on the record. What, I said, in case he does something else? You're scaring me. It was an odd comment coming from me because throughout everything that happened over the past several months, even including the ill-fated telephone hurl, I would never really describe my feelings about Jimmy and the divorce process as having any element of fear involved. I was aware that he had told his friends that it was him who had left me, and I really was OK with that. If he needed people to believe that he had walked away, it was fine. I didn't care about blame or pride and was willing to allow any spin that he wanted to put on the break up. Perhaps he even believed it himself. Who knew what he believed.

But I have to say the vicious cut in my cable wire gave me pause. Why? Maybe he didn't do it. But if he had, that kind of displaced anger disturbed me. Had he thought that I wasn't serious? Did the arrival of the filing papers as visible testimony to my intent enrage him enough to do this? When did he do it? I tried to think of the last time I watched that TV and thought it was maybe Thursday evening when I sat at my kitchen table not eating my dinner. We checked the other TVs and each was working--but cutting the cable to them would have required a ladder which Jimmy surely knew. I didn't know what to think, but I took Bella's advice and called the police to report it. Then I called the cable company and they kindly sent out a repairman later in the afternoon. That evening as we sat at the kitchen table eating our pizza and watching the news, I was aware that the divorce had quite possibly entered a new phase. And I was, indeed, vaguely afraid.

CHAPTER 12

Although it hardly seemed possible or even appropriate, spring arrived with the special glory it always has in our town. Early promises of the beauty to come start with the snow drops, the crocus, the daffodils and the forsythia, stubbornly blooming in March and April, no matter what frigid temperatures or even untimely snowfalls come to plague us. Then, all of a sudden, we have the cherry blossoms, profusely visible as the cherry trees that line the town's main road create two or three miles of breathtaking pale pink arches. Within May we also have first, the azalea, which do well in our acidic soil, and then, later in May, the lush rhododendrons. The grass starts to green, the sprinklers start to spritz the lawns, and the trees shyly show their brand new delicate greenery. The nurseries open for business and everyone plants. Window boxes, large and luscious container pots, and flower beds are filled with the annuals that will radiate color all summer long. The hydrangea and other flowering shrubs leaf out and prepare to bloom, as well. All of this always seems like some great recurring miracle to me.

A great deal of nothing was happening on the divorce front. Jimmy had requested and gotten an extension for the deadline to respond to the court regarding the filing. I came to understand he could possibly do this again and maybe even again without serious legal challenge. I thought I would simply hunker down and wait him out. I was still unable to understand why, in the face of his new *amore* in Canada, delay would be to his advantage, but I was beyond expecting either logical or consistent behavior from him. There were legal maneuvers we could have undertaken to try to force the matter along, but my small bud of fear, repressed as much as possible, and the beautiful blooming of spring, for whatever reasons, moved me to chose to wait. *When in doubt, do nothing.* Both my friend Eileen and Dr. Waxman seemed to think this was, if not wonderful, at least acceptable. Both knew that waiting and doing nothing were two of the hardest things in the world for me to do and so I think they accepted that it took a great deal of effort on my part to do so.

So just as I was almost relaxing into my new wait-and-see posture, enjoying the mild weather, ending my semester at the college, and starting to play some golf in the new spring sunshine, something quite terrible happened. I got a call late one Friday afternoon from Jimmy's daughter Christie. Telling me that Jimmy was in jail. My fucking father's been arrested, is what she said. I could hear the trembling in her voice and I didn't know if it was anger or tears or both. What for, I asked? Then she really started rambling and crying and it took a long time to sort out the story which, after a long period of stops and starts and mixed messages, I got.

Apparently Gabrielle, the love of his life in Canada, had broken things off, whatever those things had been, but Jimmy, not one to take *no* for an answer, had been attempting to see her anyway. She subsequently got a restraining order--or something they called a Peace Order in Canada--which Jimmy had thoroughly violated (by parking his rented car across the street from her apartment and sitting there for what was apparently a very long time) and so was arrested in Canada for violating the Peace Order. Christie didn't know the ins and outs of the Canadian legal system but for whatever reason, bail had been denied and Jimmy was sitting in a Canadian prison awaiting a judicial hearing, the penalties for violating the order including both a fine and/ or up to six months in prison. Jimmy had apparently been informed of the Peace Order and its terms (served with papers in his hotel room), but decided to sit in his car and stare at Gabrielle's windows anyway. After several hours, she apparently called the police. They approached his car and told him to leave and he did, but then within an hour or so came back again. After another hour, Gabrielle called the police again and this time, they took Jimmy in.

Oh God, I thought, admittedly focusing at first more on what this would mean for my divorce than any feelings of largesse toward Jimmy or his jailhouse future. I asked Christie all the obvious questions--did he have a lawyer, were his friends helping (to which she replied what friends?), did the rest of his family know? I was finally able to ascertain that John, perhaps his only remaining active friend, had gotten a lawyer in Canada to represent him and that John was also somehow attempting to appeal to Gabrielle to drop the charges, apparently using Jimmy's fragile mental state as a leveraging argument. But everything was still up in the air or nowhere and Christie was going to fly up to Canada the next morning to meet John and see what they could do together. She said she'd call me the next day and I tried to offer whatever reassurances I could muster. Somewhere very deep inside I felt incredibly pained for poor, dear, lost Jimmy. But I was also deeply afraid for what impact this would have on my divorce and, to say the least, increasingly frustrated.

Meanwhile I called Gabe, my lawyer, who was out but called back about a half hour later, a half hour during which my blood pressure must have soared. Gabe just groaned when I told him of Jimmy's circumstance and then, after a pause, said he would see how this might affect the status of the divorce in any way, good, bad, or not at all. It seemed logical to me that the local courts might not been inclined to continue to extend deadlines to a felon, but Gabe said it wasn't that easy. He asked if I could get the name of the lawyer who was representing Jimmy, that he'd call him and see if they somehow could "work something out."

I was going to call Lee, just to have someone to vent to, but then thought better of it. The fewer people in my town who knew about this, the better. Instead, I called Eileen, asked if I could come over for a glass of wine, and then drove off into the beautiful spring sunshine to what had become that primary place of refuge--Eileen's farm and the comfort of her friendship. She was outside with the dogs when I arrived--her two little Daschunds, foraging around in the spring grass for whatever prey struck their fancy. Eileen was in her usual khaki pants and L. L. Bean vest worn over a long-sleeved t-shirt. Her short, thick blond hair was lifted a little by the breeze and her high color indicated that she was just ending a long trek through her fields with the dogs. She hustled me into the house and took out the chilled bottle of white wine, ever present in her fridge. She poured and we lit cigarettes and I told her the latest little episode in this ongoing soap opera that was my life.

Really, I concluded, I don't know how this affects the divorce situation and while I keep hoping that his new-found criminal status could be to my advantage, I have a feeling that this will just add another layer of delay. I mean, you hear all the time about how people divorce spouses who have been sent to prison, but I just don't know how that works. Do criminals lose their right to contest a divorce? Plus, I said, what if he pleads insanity or whatever they call it and then has to go to a mental hospital. I cannot even imagine what that might entail. I was rambling. I didn't know the law in general, I didn't know Canadian law in particular, I was just swimming in ignorance and outlandish speculation. Well, Eileen said, I don't think he could ever be found legally insane--which means not knowing the difference between right and wrong. I mean, surely he knew that sitting in front of her apartment house was in violation of the restraining order, no matter how cuckoo he might be. Just wait, she said. And I knew that indeed that was my only choice. Yes, I said, wait and try not to jump out of my skin. Have more wine, Eileen said. So I did.

The next day, Saturday, Christie called me in the early evening and said that Jimmy was still in jail awaiting the judiciary hearing scheduled for the following Wednesday.

She had been allowed a brief visit. He's almost catatonic, Christie told me, and has thus far been totally useless in assisting his lawyer. The advice was to throw himself on the mercy of the court, plead something like extreme emotional distress following the break up of the romance (which no one yet fully understood, Gabrielle claiming that there had been no "romance," only a few dates). He can barely talk, Christie said. It's just so disgusting and pathetic. They took his glasses and no one can find them and he can't read anything or even see a lot about his surroundings. I didn't know whether to hug him or slap him she said through her tears. He's not eating and keeps swearing at the people around him--the guards and court officers. It's like he's had a total mental breakdown. But he could be faking the whole goddamned thing--who ever knows?

My heart was in my throat through most of this conversation but I tried to sound calm for Christie, telling her that I was sure his state of mind was temporary, whatever its cause, and that he was probably in some kind of shock which would pass. Just see if you can get him to eat, maybe even find some way to get him a Valium or Prozac or something to help him cope with the anxiety. She thought he might have some Valium among his toiletries in his hotel room and that maybe she could smuggle one or two into him. The security isn't all that tight, she said. What about his lawyer, I asked? Does he seem competent? He seems sort of bored, Christie said, like it's no big deal. So, I said, maybe he doesn't think Jimmy will get jail time, I asked? More like he doesn't give a damn, she said. What does John think, I asked? Well, she said, I think he's trying to stay calm for me, but I think he's really worried underneath. And my father just doesn't seem to get it, you know? I knew.

Later that night I worried myself into a shallow, restless sleep. I had dreams that seemed to be staged at the foot of my bed about men in chains, prisoners in orange suits, and guards pushing them here and there and finally, finally I forced myself awake. I shook off the covers, got up, and walked to my bedroom window, looking out on my peaceful street with its muted street lamps, the pavement glazed with dampness. Apparently it had rained while I had been tossing and turning inside a prison of my own making. In a sense, my dream had been not only a version of Jimmy's plight but an apt metaphor for my own.

I went to the kitchen, heated up some milk in the microwave, added sugar, and sat there sipping, trying not to think. Finally, I was able to go back to bed and fall into an exhausted sleep. I did not dream, or if I did, I forgot it.

CHAPTER 13

I didn't hear anything more for days. I resisted the temptation of calling Christie, although she had given me the number at her hotel. I thought it better if I waited for her to call me and, I think, I didn't want any more nightmare-inspiring conversations. My heartburn was back. I wasn't talking about Jimmy's incident to anyone, refused the temptation of telling Bella and getting the comfort of the relief that I knew talking with her would bring. Not fair, I kept saying. Do not unload on your daughter's life. She had been so kind and supportive that I could barely think of her without crying. But enough was enough. I would not pull her into this drama until Act Three was over. I'd probably tell her, but not until I knew how the story ended. I had spoken to Eileen, but only to tell her that I hadn't heard anything more.

This was the final week of the semester, the third week in May, and I was therefore busy with term papers and final grades. This was wonderfully distracting for me and I can say that the days did not drag. The weight of Jimmy's situation was something I was able to push away and only feel intermittently tugging at my consciousness. So when the telephone rang that next Saturday morning, three days following the appointed judiciary hearing, I was not particularly apprehensive. It briefly crossed my mind that this would be Christie, but it wasn't. It was Jimmy.

So, I'm home, he started. Better than in jail, I answered. Are you free? I'm free, was all he said. And then, after a long pause during which I could hear him taking some deep breaths, he said free at last; he said I paid the money, listened to the speech, and got free. I don't think I'd better go back to Canada for a while, but it's over. I just thought I'd tell you. Christie shouldn't have gotten you involved in the first place; I'm sorry for that. But I just wanted to tell you myself that it's over. Well, I said, congratulations, I guess. Yeah, he said. Well John and that fucking lawyer saved my ass. Congratulate them. You know, I said. I'm really sorry. I mean that. And he said, I know you do. And then he said, I signed the papers and sent them back to your lawyer yesterday. Oh wow, I said, before I had the time to think that this remark was probably not appropriate. So you'll be rid of me soon, he continued--all of this in a strange, dull tone of voice. Jimmy, look, I said. It didn't work. That's all. No blame, no fault. It just didn't work. OK? Sure, OK, he said and hung up.

I stood next to the telephone for a long time and what I was feeling, I think, was sadness most of all. Somewhere behind the sadness was a small hope that perhaps it was truly over, but suddenly *over* felt like a lonely place to be. *Over* felt like failure and loss and tears. And so I finally took Dr. Waxman's advice and cried. I was seeing us at our sad little wedding ceremony, both of us smiling, filled with a hope that was probably dead long before we said I do. I was hearing Jimmy introduce me to someone--this is my wife; I don't think you've met. I was thinking of Jimmy sitting in a bar after we separated, alone, handing out his business cards to women saying, call me, I'm getting divorced.

So, no matter how much you want something, you always find that you really want something else. You want it to have worked. That's what you really want.

CHAPTER 14

What you also learn is that nothing is ever really over. There is no punctuation that ends it, no timer that runs out and beeps at you. Whatever happens to you is forever and even though the circumstances change and legal papers dissolve certain arrangements, it is never over. It is part of you forever. I suppose I really knew that all along.

After that call from Jimmy in late May, I did nothing relevant to his call for the rest of the weekend. I went back to doing my final grades, finished on Sunday, posted the grades on the official forms, and drove the forms to campus early Monday morning. It was a beautiful near-summer day and the campus looked brilliant in the May sunshine. Ours was a relatively new campus, well-designed around a central quadrangle, all symmetrical red brick buildings with trees that had twenty-five years growth on them, trees that filled in what used to be a lot of empty spaces. I had been at the college from its beginning. I started as a part-time instructor on the day the new campus opened. Previous to that, classes had met in various buildings downtown, but I didn't work for the college then. I started when the campus did. I think of that briefly as I walk to the Registrar's office in the Administration Building to hand in the official grades that would become part of dozens of official transcripts, for better or for worse. My sad little band of remedial students did not fare well. Only six of them passed with a C or better, two got D grades, and the rest had just faded away. I thought I had done the best that I could do for them, but I'll never really know. You try. That's all.

I lingered for a while in the Registrar's office, talking with some other faculty members who were also turning in grades. It was a euphoric time for us. We worked hard for the fifteen weeks of the semester, spending fifty or sixty hours a week teaching, reading, researching, writing lectures, grading, meeting students, always with hopes for success for all, never fully realizing those hopes, of course. But when the grades were in, it was over and summer beckoned with its long light fingers. Some faculty taught during the summer months, but I never did. I luxuriated in sleeping late, going to the beach for long lazy days, playing golf, going to parties, taking little trips within the region. People spend a lot of money to come to the Jersey shore to vacation in the summer, but I live here. It's different when you live here. It's better.

I bid everyone farewell with always the same wishes--have a great summer--and then stopped at my office to tidy it up for its summer break. I filled a briefcase with some unfinished business that I could attend to at home, re-shelved books, filed or discarded what seemed like several pounds of paper, watered my plants, left a note for the department secretary asking that she water them over the summer, and then walked back to the parking lot and drove away. It was a fairly good bet that I wouldn't be back until the last two weeks of August prior to the fall term. The year in academic terms runs from September to May and our New Year's Eve is the day we turn the grades in. *Vale*!

When I got home, I made some calls. I 'phoned and updated Eileen on Jimmy's release and she was relieved on my behalf. I agreed with her that things could turn on a dime, especially when dealing with someone as volatile as Jimmy, but we both just finally said fingers crossed and promised to see each other soon. Then I called Bella at work and gave her a very quick summary of events. I told her the end first so that she wouldn't have to hear the details in suspense. Like Eileen, she said, one day at a time, you know him. I agreed, but something inside me believed that this time it was different, that it was over. I know this is also what I wanted to believe, but I did nonetheless believe it.

Then I called Christie. She was strangely reticent. I had expected an outpouring of details related to her trip to Canada, which is why I put off her call until last, but she said very little at first and then just said that she and her Dad had had a disagreement on Sunday and so she had flown back home later that day, not staying for the judicial hearing. But I guess he did all right, she concluded. Well, I said, he's home. I think he had to pay a fine and is apparently *persona non gratis* in Canada, whatever that means, but apparently no jail time. Yeah, she said, the bastard always manages to land on his feet. I know, I said, but the complications of some other outcome would have been horrific for us all, so better he land on his feet this time. I think John gave him the money for the fine, Christie said, and I said I wouldn't be surprised, that John was a friend and very concerned for Jimmy's welfare. But you know, she said, there should just come a day when he actually has to pay for what he does with money or time or something. I tried to persuade her that a strong desire for payback was not a great ingredient for a meaningful relationship. I also told her that justice was often imperfect or non-existent and therefore a tough measure for contentment in life. She said, I hear you, but I doubt that she did.

I unpacked my briefcase and organized my desk for summer, making little piles of papers on my now very neat desk. I made one small pile for things I had to finish within the week, one pile for things I had to start in early August preparatory for returning to school, and then one pile of summer-long projects that had to be tackled a little at a time. According to an old rule of life and work, I understood that I would do the immediate work within the next few days and then not look at the other piles at all for a full three weeks until well after Memorial Day. Doing nothing for those weeks was the little prize I gave myself at the end of each academic year. Finally, I wandered in to my bedroom, my neat piles of summer work having been constructed, and lay down on my bed. I began to think with a new mind, thinking beyond the divorce and what I might do with my new peace. I thought about selling the house and knew almost immediately that I would do it, not right away, but possibly the following spring. The house was as good as it was going to get, the gardens finally thriving and the holes in the furnishings left by Jimmy's departure filled in as much as I wanted them filled. But the house was still going to be an emotional burden, I knew that. Not only was this big house with its four bedrooms too big for me, it was filled with things that I wanted to get away from, not exactly memories, but surely associations, ghosts, emanations, whatever. Ironically, given Jimmy's characterizations, it would never be *my* house. It wasn't a house that embraced me or charmed me, it never had been, and now it was just a place to live, a little too big, a little too boring.

I also thought about social constructs and ways in which I would live my life as a single person. In reality, I had been doing this for months already, but since so much of my time had been spent embroiled in the dramas of the divorce, I didn't really count these months as transformative. I lived, had chosen to live, in what had to be seen as a "couples" town, or at least couples comprised the social strata in which I dwelled. All my friends and acquaintances, with few exceptions, were solidly married people with children and sometimes grandchildren and this very married condition structured their lives, what they did and who they saw. In fact, it was this solidarity that I sought when I moved back to town. And now, I finally realized, I was or would soon become an outsider, no longer a person who qualified for membership in the couples' world. This realization came as something of a surprise to me. My friends had been enormously supportive during the separation process, but as this smoothed out and became history, when I was no longer a couple for months and then years, I just knew there would be things from which I would be excluded because I did not have a partner. This had happened to me when I had been widowed ten years before, so it was odd that when faced with it again I should be surprised at all. There is a price for everything. People were enormously kind to me when my first husband was killed and, at first, inclusive. But, eventually, vacations were planned, golf foursomes set up, tables for holiday parties secured (with an even number of places) and countless other casual couples events transpired from which I was excluded. I never found this either cruel or intentional. I knew how things worked. Hell, I had done the same things myself--when my husband was alive, when I was married to Jimmy. If the party was big enough, I might be invited (and encouraged to bring "a guest"), but the smaller dinner parties or outings consisted of couples only. It never entered anyone's mind to include a single woman, no matter how much they liked her.

And then, of course, I worked. I was the only one of my close women friends who had a full-time job and although I was free to play all summer, I was never available during the week after Labor Day through late May and so did no women's clubs or bridge games or tennis groups or theater outings. Occasionally, I ducked out of work to meet friends for a birthday luncheon and still had weekends free to socialize, but I wasn't ever a full-time member of the women's culture. I tried to "have it all," work, family, social life, and I succeeded fairly well. But now having lost a mate twice, I was just different, that's all. I didn't now or ever feel either regret or self-pity about this. It was what it was. No one gets it all.

I must have fallen asleep with my thoughts because the next thing I knew, the telephone beside my bed was ringing and, as I looked at the clock, saw that it was almost four o'clock. I answered the phone a bit sleepily and it was Gabe, my lawyer, telling me he had gotten the paperwork from Jimmy. He said that everything seemed to be in order so that the filing was now complete and that what we needed next was a court date, pretty much a waiting game until our number came up. He thought we'd hear from the court in about six weeks and that the court date might be scheduled for about two to three months following that. It sounded like an eternity to me, but Gabe was very upbeat, acknowledged that he was relieved, and advised me to put everything out of my mind, get on with life, and that when matters were finalized, it would seem like no time at all. Easy for you to say, I thought, but never said anything except thank you and keep in touch. I had a fleeting thought that Gabe would really be thrilled when he was done with me, and who would blame him? But then I thought, conversely, that if my business was the most difficult he ever encountered, he'd be lucky. Well, maybe excepting that little assault issue with my drunken lothario several years back.

CHAPTER 15

The next Tuesday, I was at the club having a late lunch after our weekly golf game. I didn't notice until someone pointed him out to me, but sitting at a table near the windows with a group of what looked like professional associates was one of the men whom I had dated during my break from Jimmy, before we got married, the one who, when we were out somewhere, looked at everyone in the room but me. He was an attractive man, not conventionally handsome, but tallish, very well-groomed in a conservative way, immaculate, dark hair, slightly balding, with an impish kind of face that seemed at once very serious and yet ever-poised for an elusive smile. He was generally well-liked but had kept pretty much to himself after his first divorce a dozen years before which had created a small scandal in town--some infidelity thing that I had never really gotten details about. He was, coincidentally, socially friendly with my Dean at the college--one of those Friday night out with the boys friendships. His ex-wife and her new husband had been to a couple of parties that I had attended, but I wasn't really friendly with either. My Dean occasionally mentioned Adam to me, knowing we were acquainted, but otherwise our paths never crossed after our aborted dating period five years before, about three months of mixed messages and promises not kept. There had been no animosity, however, and then I married Jimmy whom I was now about to un-marry.

Adam and his party got up to leave the dining room and on his way out, he detoured past our table to say hello to a few women he knew and to me. Khaki summer suit, red tie, brilliantly white shirt, subtle musk smell. He looked good. He put his hand on the back of my chair, leaned over, and said in a quiet voice to me that he had heard about my divorce, asked how everything was going. A little better, I said, I *think*. and I laughed. One day at a time, he said--why did everyone say that--and then said he'd give me a call, maybe we could have dinner. I'd like that, I said. But his parting line was always that he'd give me a call and, so often, he hadn't. The women at the table who knew we had dated gave me a look, but I just waved my hand, the "whatever" wave that summed up my impression of the encounter. Good old Adam, I said, and changing the subject, went back to my turkey sandwich.

But, surprisingly, he did call a few days later and we made a date for dinner on Saturday night. He suggested we eat at the club and I said, fine, sounds good. When I thought about that later, I wondered why he wanted to take me to a place where both of us were so well known, where our date would surely attract attention and get mentioned by people who knew us. When we had dated before, we had rarely gone to the club, never on a Saturday night, and so this was new. I was thinking that maybe he needed to make some kind of public statement like, hey, I'm dating again, good for me, and I was as useful a prop as any. When we had dated previously, I had offered very little drama, so I suppose I was comfortable, non-threatening, available. I recalled that he had gotten engaged some time after Jimmy and I had gotten married. I had heard that he and his fiancée had broken up, reconciled, and then broken up again for good. I seemed to remember that the woman was quite a bit younger than him, but I wasn't certain. I really couldn't recall the time frames for all this romantic activity and gossip and, given my current overwhelming cynicism about all things romantic, didn't care. The date was a meal, something to do. At best, I'd get semi-ignored and, in between, have some good conversation with Adam who was bright, amusing, and interesting. There were worse things I could be doing on a Saturday night.

This thinking led me to consider the whole issue of me being the subject of town gossip. I recalled Lee's comments that night we had drinks and dinner when she alluded to "everyone" talking about parts of my life, my problems. I didn't give it much credence, then; hardly thought my paltry little divorce--ending a short-term second marriage, with no children and not much real scandal attached--would be of much interest on the gossip scale. It suddenly occurred to me that I'd been naive to believe that I was somehow operating privately, that what was happening was just not seen or talked about by others, that I lived in some kind of protected bubble. I tried to imagine what types of conversations might have been taking place. Some of my friends disliked or disapproved of Jimmy, mostly because of his rather salacious reputation, sometimes because of his attitude which on occasion could be unpleasantly arrogant or cold. Some of my friends liked him or found him amusing. I don't know. Maybe people said she never should have married him. They'd have been right. Maybe they said she's better off without him. Maybe people said they knew it would never work. Right, right. The more I rehearsed all the possible conversations in which my divorce was the subject, the less I cared. So why bother with what people would say when I appeared with Adam Saturday night? I just refused to be self-conscious about it.

But when Adam and I got to the club Saturday night I *did* feel a bit self-conscious at first, in spite of myself. I had dressed carefully with some strategies in mind--hoping to be conservative, low key, attempting to match Adam's style, wearing nothing to attract attention. A plain black linen sleeveless dress, some chunky pearls, low black heels, my hair pulled back in a clip, a large red purse to avoid looking as if I were going to a funeral. But as soon as we arrived, I could feel the *maitre de* looking at us with interest as he greeted us formally, eyebrows lightly raised, a small smile playing at his mouth, trying to look normal as he showed us to our table. He knew who we were, of course, as members, and probably knew more about us than I had ever before considered: All this *knowing* about me by people! I glanced across the crowd in the dining room without making direct eye contact with anyone. The room was quite crowded, but I didn't recognize anyone I knew well and then I simply started to focus on Adam as a defense against the *knowing*, smiling, getting settled at the table, getting menus, ordering a cocktail, and then pleased to find ourselves in a sort of sheltered alcove instead, thank goodness, of being placed somewhere in the middle of the room. There was a huge palm plant to Adam's left that partially obscured his view of the room and he was also seated slanted toward me rather than toward the dining room. Perhaps this would curb his habit of looking anywhere but at me, I thought, sardonically, and then checked myself. Whatever was going on with this dinner, I didn't care. I was out on a date on a Saturday night, a long time since that had happened, and I was going to enjoy whatever I could about it.

And I did. The cocktails were just right, tart vodka gimlets, the food excellent and there was something comfortable about it all. Adam and I were hardly strangers or strange with each other. We didn't have to play at getting to know each other or at editing out all the preferably forgotten aspects of our lives. He knew, I knew, enough, if not everything, to have long since gotten over that hump. We could ask after each other's children with enough knowledge about who they were to be truly interested in the answers. We could talk about friends we had in common. We didn't care about each other's past marriages or romances, so there was no tension if a mention was made of "my wife" or "my husband" as our conversation progressed. Adam didn't gaze over his shoulder at the room--perhaps because of the palm plant, perhaps because he wasn't too interested in who was there or who was looking or who he should look at.

After we lingered over an after-dinner drink at the bar, he drove me home and I asked if he'd like to come in for coffee. He accepted, and we drank our coffee and had a friendly, confiding kind of conversation about our latest break-ups. He had, in fact, been engaged, un-engaged, re-engaged and then finally not engaged forever to the same woman over a four-year time span, their final split coming about a year before. He was careful not to name her--I doubt that I knew her anyway--or to say anything revealing or personal or nasty about her. He was gentlemanly and kept the conversation focused on himself with some mildly rueful irony directed at what he now saw as his own naive expectations for the relationship. In fact, he said, she was just too young for me, not exactly May-December, you know, but a different generation, a whole different set of definitions and expectations. As for my part of the conversation, I just generally emphasized the whole lack of drama with regard to my situation with Jimmy--had this urge to de-mystify the process, to convert it into basics, to *irreconcilable differences* which I realized, as I spoke, that it was. That was exactly what it was, boiled down to its essence. Minus the pain, Jimmy's often neurotic behavior, the hopes gone awry, the striving and failing on my part, the final strain of the previous six months, I could see for the first time truly what was meant by "irreconcilable differences" and found enormous comfort in this, a comfort that allowed me to speak about my split from Jimmy more objectively than I think I ever had. Adam was a good listener and I think this, too, was very helpful to me in de-coding my emotions, finding a place for them even outside of this conversation.

At one point Adam remarked that my home was charming and I was inspired to tell him a few stories about how it got the way it was, charming or not. He was particularly aghast at the tale of the felonious interior decorator and asked me why in the world I hadn't reported her to the police. You know, I said, I never even thought of it, not that it would have done any good or gotten back my money that I was sure had been long gone. But, in reality, I said, it was just one item in a long continuum of horrors that seemed to be part of the pattern of my life then. I mean, I said, I think I just saw it as part of my fate rather than as a crime. Does that make sense, I asked? Yeah, he said, in a kind of odd way, it does. But it shouldn't have.

After the coffee was done, I walked Adam to the door, holding his hand as we walked, and when we got to the door, he leaned over and kissed me. It was not our first kiss; we had actually had a few brief but pleasant sexual encounters during our dating experience five years before, but this was not a truly passionate kiss, not a start of something kiss. It was pleasant, friendly, intimate and somehow trusting, reassuring. Thanks, I said, pulling back, I had a really nice evening. Me too, he said. And then unfortunately he added: I'll call you.

CHAPTER 16

In fact, Adam did call me and we went out together several more times in late May and during the month of June, once or twice a week. It remained casual with, again, one or two brief sexual interludes. We were comfortable in bed together and I was reasonably secure in the belief that this was not the start of an extended affair, was not going anywhere, and would not survive the summer. In fact, Adam had a second home in South Carolina at a golf resort and a large fishing boat, both of which took a lot of his time and attention. I was, at the time, examining the idea of what was then considered a new romantic phenomenon called "casual sex," meaning engaging in sexual activity without the accompaniment of declared love, engagement, or any of the trappings of romance. As archaic as this seems now in the age of "hook-ups" with near-strangers, casual sex was truly thought to be a new chapter in the moral/sexual history of our culture thirty years ago. Articles were being written, talk shows were focusing on the topic, and by the time I finally realized that this phenomenon probably included my relationship with Adam, the relationship ended and I would have plenty of time to think about whether or not I was morally comfortable with casual sex. At the time, since I was planning never to fall "in love" again, I seemed to have two choices: casual sex or no sex at all.

One of our dates near the end of June was our attendance at a super-gala party thrown by a huge accounting firm for all of its premier clients. It was staged at a park in north Jersey, Liberty Park, which looks across the Hudson River to the Manhattan skyline, the party itself in a massive old railroad station that had been restored as an historical site. It was truly a gala affair--cocktails available at the "ticket booths," never-ending hors d'oevres, both passed and set on tables throughout, dancing, and a sit-down roast-beef dinner with extravagant dessert tables and designer coffees available after dinner. I barely saw Adam during the cocktail hour as he was working the rooms for whatever reason. But as I strolled around the old station, crowd-watching, nibbling, drinking a martini, I ran into a friend of Jimmy's, Howard McIntosh, who was apparently one of the premier clients invited to the party.

We chatted casually, carefully staying away from the Jimmy topic for a while until Howard eventually asked if I had heard that Jimmy was in hospital with suspected heart problems. I hadn't heard--hadn't spoken to either Christie or John since the Canada affair-- and so I followed up a little, tactfully pressing Howard for more details. It was the familiar story of chest-pains and follow-up tests until Howard chuckled a little and said Jimmy had apparently created something of a scene in the hospital, refusing to stay in bed, walking the halls holding high his IV and demanding to see his doctor, threatening to leave the hospital if he couldn't, all of this in the wee hours of the morning, Jimmy's hospital gown flapping and revealing his naked posterior to the amused nurses. Supposedly one of the nurses was frightened, called security, and then Jimmy was finally sedated and put back to bed. I so much wanted to tell Howard that this was not just another Jimmy scandal story, part of the urban legend, but that in fact the poor man was clearly battling some sort of mental illness and that someone better diagnose and treat this soon before Jimmy truly went seriously off the rails. There was, however, no point in saying any of this to Howard since he could obviously do nothing about it and the end result would just probably be a new gossip headline in the Jimmy saga: Estranged wife calls soon-to-be-ex-hubby crazy. I resolved to call Christie, or maybe John, the next day, breaking my vow of silence until I had a divorce decree in hand. After all, if Jimmy had some kind of serious break down, that wouldn't exactly be good for the divorce either, would it? Howard also said that he had heard that Jimmy was about to move to Florida. I hadn't heard this either.

I have to say that I was worried. Vague thoughts of a further delay of our divorce proceedings either because of Jimmy's alleged heart problems or of his alleged flight to Florida began to bring on feelings of panic. When Adam finally rejoined me at our table for dinner, he sensed my mood and began to apologize for his extended absence. No, I almost shouted, not that at all. I'll tell you later. I distracted myself by conversing with the others at our table, getting a waiter to bring me a glass of Pino Noir, and focusing on salad, soup, and beef. After dinner, Adam and I cruised the dessert tables, sampled some, had our coffee, and then decided to get the car and leave the party before the inevitable mass exodus and interminable wait for the parking valets to deliver cars.

On the ride home, to explain my earlier mood, I gave Adam an abbreviated version of Jimmy's latest exploits as told by Howard, leaving out the mental illness part, which I never felt comfortable talking about except with John or Christie. Adam was kind with his responses, more interested in calming me than in providing an objective analysis, I think, but whatever he was doing, it worked and I did feel calmer, just because in the telling, things didn't sound so bad. Jimmy probably did not have a heart problem, or at least not a serious one, and planning to move to Florida did not mean imminent departure. Possibly his plan was to leave after the divorce--because it would take time to sell his condo up here and find someplace to go in Florida. He had mentioned to me several times during the course of our marriage that he'd like to retire to Florida. His context for this desire was the immediate future. He was in his late fifties at that time and thought retirement was imminent, in a few years' time, while I was in my mid-forties, retirement a long way off, in my mind. I liked to get away to Florida for a few weeks in the winter, but the thought of living there permanently bored me to distraction. For me, thoughts of retirement were twenty years away at the least. I liked my job, and even if I retired from the job, I liked my town, my friends, had little desire to leave them behind for any extended period of time. It hadn't really become a point of friction between us, however, perhaps because Jimmy thought I'd just go along with his plans in a few years' time.

By the time we got home from the party, Adam and my conversation had drifted to other matters. Because it was late and I think we were both tired, I didn't invite him in nor did he make any move to extend the evening beyond my front door. After thank yous and a brief kiss, we parted on my doorstep with Adam saying, as ever, he'd call me. This time, however, he didn't.

Meanwhile, the next day I called John. He told me that in fact Jimmy's cardiac tests were all normal, he was out of the hospital, and he probably had had some kind of indigestion or perhaps a panic attack. So that was a relief. He also said that Jimmy had been in Florida for a week at the beginning of the month and that, yes, he had been looking at propterties in the same area that John and his wife had recently bought a winter home. To John's knowledge, Jimmy had no imminent move planned. But he thought that eventually, Jimmy would move down there, perhaps before the winter set in again up here. I didn't say, but thought, that would be OK. I had October in mind as the settlement of our divorce, based on what Gabe had said about the time frames. John and I talked briefly but inconclusively about Jimmy seeing some kind of psychologist, but John was cautious with his comments, more evasive than he had been in the past, and so I didn't pursue it. I trusted that John would not let Jimmy go stark raving mad right before his eyes and I could tell he did have eyes on. So I let it go. I called Christie, but she was out, so I left a non-urgent message for her to call me when she had time and then hung up the phone on my anxiety. I couldn't dwell on the possibilities any longer. There were just too many. I repressed.

A few days passed and when I didn't hear from Adam, I debated calling him. I had invited him to accompany me to a July Fourth party to be held at the home of friends of mine who lived on the river, a nice vantage point from which to watch the annual fireworks supplied by the famous Grucci brothers, always a grand show. He had accepted the invite, but we hadn't confirmed it or talked about pick-up times. The party was now about a week away. I had accepted the invitation and indicated to my hostess that Adam would be coming with me, so I felt kind of pressed about confirming plans with him. But I didn't call and waited. When the party was three days away, and I still hadn't heard from him, I finally just said--OK, call. After all, it was my invite. Perhaps he was waiting for me to follow up.

I called, but there was no answer, so I left a message asking him to call me to confirm plans for the party. He didn't call back. The day before the party, I called again, got no answer, left no message, and went to the party alone. That was, for all intents and purposes, the end of Adam. I understand that this ghosting-out behavior is now becoming a common mode of dumping an unwanted companion, but back then, it was just another form of extraordinarily rude behavior, a way of ignoring the humanity of another, of hiding behind silence, considered neither clever nor civil.

I wasn't heart-broken or embarrassed. I was angry. I found it so unforgivably ill-mannered, so inexplicably discourteous, that I just couldn't get it out of my head for days. For a few weeks, I would make up excuses for his silence--a faulty answering machine, illness, illness in the family, a business emergency, something or anything that might explain the lack of communication. I debated calling again to ask him just why he was being so intolerably rude, but just couldn't justify it--I didn't want to sound as if I were the dumped and dejected lover because I wasn't--and so I moved on, anger still below the surface, questions galore (was it something I said?), but did nothing. I mentioned it once to a good friend who was also friends with Adam, but she sort of blew it off, made it seem inconsequential with a sort of shit-happens flippancy. I agreed that shit happens and that I had not expected a long-term commitment. Some manners would have been nice, however, I added. She seemed to be laughing at me and so I just finally let the entire matter drop, never said anything more. Occasionally, someone would ask me how Adam was and I'd just say, gee, I don't know. I haven't seen him for a while. Years later, I was reminded of Adam's behavior and amused by Glenn Close's performance as she portrayed a jilted one-night stand lover in the movie *Fatal Attraction*. Her famous line--*I won't be ignored*--led to a dead bunny, family pet, and an almost dead Michael Douglas (the offending lover). Of course, Glenn Close was portrayed as a mad woman in the film. Indeed. How could any *sane* woman expect a man not to use her and discard her at will?

Months later, this is what I learned about Adam: The woman he had had the affair with years before, the affair that had broken up his first marriage, had suddenly become available--as a result of the death of her husband who had apparently been ill for a long time. Her husband had died in April before Adam and I started dating again in May and I suppose they had been observing a "decent" mourning period before beginning to see each other again. I extrapolated that I had been Adam's coming out party, his public re-socialization before reuniting with his true love, which he did in September. They subsequently lived together for a few years and then got married, even though I recall Adam once saying, if I ever decide to get married again, shoot me. Whatever. No one likes being used, especially as she awaits a divorce that seems at times as if it will never happen. Why July 1 was my dump date, I'll never know. Why I didn't deserve an honest explanation--or any explanation, honest or dishonest--I'll never know. What I do know is that this entire experience lent a whole new meaning for me to the term "casual sex," adding a kind of connotative sub text that screamed, "sex--with absolutely no strings attached, not even to etiquette or common courtesy." As a result, the concept seemed chauvinistic to me and lost its appeal. What I didn't notice at the time was how awful I felt about being dumped by someone I did not even love and how this feeling might apply to how Jimmy might be feeling, Jimmy whom I assume loved me. As the poet said, the art of losing is *very* hard to master. And, one might add: Under any circumstances.

I wondered, for example, how Adam, waiting to reunite with the woman he eventually married, could have wanted to have sex with me. My motives were relatively uncomplicated, but what might his have been? Perhaps, after all, he had no real plans to reunite with this woman when he slept with me and I was just a handy, uncomplicated sex partner. I rather hoped this was the case. As angry as I was, I still rather liked Adam and didn't really want to believe he had cheated on this woman with me--even before she was actually in his life again. I'm not even sure I actually understand how men define cheating. I think it's pretty simple for women. If you and I have a relationship and you have sex with another, that's cheating. I think perhaps men tend to think that it's only cheating if you get caught--otherwise, if no one finds out--it doesn't count. Maybe not. I know a man who cheated on his wife for more than thirty years. They were married, had three children and eventually grand children and yet he regularly dated and had sex with a string of different women for the greater part of his married life until he was well into his seventies. His wife never knew and then she did and she divorced him. He had wanted to stay married but continue his relations with other women, professed not to understand why his wife would not go along with this. Is there even an argument to be made here? I really don't know. Casual sex? Adultery? Serial adultery? My understanding of "casual sex" as the term was used thirty years ago was related to sex between single, unattached people; but even that seemed to demand some sort of fair play.

But the sexual/marital history of our culture is rife with infidelities--Roosevelt, Eisenhower, Kennedy, Clinton--four hugely popular leaders with adulterous proclivities are only symbols of the larger culture. In France, the keeping of a mistress is a man's birth right and the culture adapts to the practice. But in America, we still maintain the myth of marital fidelity and endlessly pretend shock and disbelief when that myth is shattered, about sixty-eight percent of the time if sex data is to be believed. Is there a better way to deal with I'm from Venus, you're from Mars or is "let's pretend" the best solution? Don't ask, don't tell?

Considered from another perspective, I don't know whether or not Jimmy was unfaithful to me. The odds are that he was--based on both national data and on Jimmy's own codas. I never really thought too much about it. It's possible, I would think--but then there were so many other things wrong with our marriage that it hardly mattered. I never found out, one way or another. It's odd that I didn't pursue the truth on this matter more vigorously. But I didn't. Because in the end, it was irrelevant.

CHAPTER 17

And so the summer passed away. There were early morning visits to the beach to sit with friends and chatter away as we all watched the sun rise high over the ocean and we all turned incredibly brown, something many of us lived to regret years later (wrinkles, skin cancer, our just rewards for an indulgence in what seemed, at the time, such a simple, innocent pleasure). There were also golf games--some tense tournaments, some fun outings to golf courses not our own--and then parties of all shapes and sizes, some of which I attended, not uncomfortably, unescorted. Once or twice, I invited male friends to accompany me--friends who would not misinterpret my motive for the invitation and would be reasonably comfortable in a gathering of relative strangers; but mostly I just sucked it up and went solo. It was OK after the first few minutes. Couples split, conversation groups formed. No one needed his or her partner to drink and talk and laugh.

And then abruptly it was mid-August, time to return to the college three days a week to take up some administrative responsibilities while the Dean of the department was on vacation, and also to "write my courses," as I called it. Sometimes I threw out previous course outlines, starting from scratch, re-inventing a course that I thought needed it.

Other times, I retained existing course outlines, revising as I thought was indicated, adding and subtracting assignments that had worked or not worked well previously, reorganizing units into what seemed to be more logical sequences. I always wanted to give my students a complete course outline at the start of the term--although I cautioned them not to get more than two weeks ahead in completing assignments (fat chance) since all were subject to change. Nonetheless, I always thought it was necessary for them to see, at least in general terms, where we were going in the course and what their responsibilities would be. No surprises for them. I lost a few kids after the first class due to this practice--the "I'm overwhelmed" syndrome. Fine. Get out while the getting's good. The kids all knew about me anyway (she's tough, a bitch, fair, demanding--whatever). They had their grapevine.

During the last two weeks in August, I went to school on Mondays, Wednesdays, and Fridays for five hours each day, played golf or beached it on Tuesdays, Thursdays, and Saturdays and really enjoyed the busyness of my weeks, taking Sundays off to read the *Times* and my current novel on my shaded deck and to watch golf on TV. I especially enjoyed staying busy during this summer and its strange combination of relaxed languishing and tense waiting to be un-married. The more hours I could fill, the fewer I had to spend doing the "waiting." At school I stayed wholly occupied with scheduling and student issues as well as with the work on my courses. On the golf course, I just cursed at the little white ball, occasionally feeling on top of the world when I actually hit a shot to where I envisioned it to be going--or when the golf gods smiled on me and allowed a skulled chip shot to wobble up to within two feet of the hole. Good luck was always welcome.

I was not a particularly good golfer and like most amateurs, could be quite awful. I had my moments however, which kept me coming back--a good shot, a good hole, and even every so often, a good round. When I played three or four times a week I could count on good holes or a good round more often. But after my first "learning experience," at about age thirty-four, I never took another lesson, and I never practiced. I rarely even hit balls before going out to play. These facts made it clear that I simply was not a truly serious player--I wasn't--and wouldn't ever get much better at the game as a result. I knew that and while on occasion wished it were different, never made the effort otherwise. When various people (like Jimmy) urged me to work more at my game, I just said that I "worked" at most everything else in my life--and that golf was not going to be one of those things. A poor excuse, but my excuse nonetheless. I think a lot of the women I played with felt about the same. And regardless, I really did love the game, no matter how frustrating it could be--or maybe even because of that. And I loved having the summers off so I could play.

But then suddenly it was Labor Day, some final summer parties crammed in over the weekend, and then the start of classes, time for my "other life" to take over. I had heard from Gabe in early August that our court date for the final decree was tentatively scheduled for October 10. He called back a week later to say that it had been moved to October 17, adding that he did not expect a further postponement.

Jimmy had agreed that the date was fine with him, so it looked like I had a firm date to circle on my calendar.

On the Tuesday after Labor Day, I played my last round of golf for the season with my regular golf group on a glorious late-summer day and confided my court date to a few friends. I had been keeping divorce details all pretty close to the vest and when asked about how things were progressing and when the big day would be, I automatically answered, fine, sometime this fall. I was somehow superstitious, feeling that if I mentioned a date, I would spook things. But over lunch with two friends on that Tuesday, I did mention October 17 and said, pray for me and then laughed. For whatever reason, the spell seemed to have lifted and with no real negative news, I thought that I could really see the light at the end of the tunnel. My friends were congratulatory and supportive.

The next day, classes started. I spent the morning chatting with colleagues, orienting some newly hired adjunct faculty members, helping students find where they were going, straightening out some erroneous class lists and room assignments and then had a quick half-sandwich at my desk. I met with my English Literature class at 2:00 PM. I had only eighteen students enrolled in this class and expected, by Friday, it would probably be down to fifteen or less. It was a course I loved to teach, Beowulf to the Neo-Classicists--a very full survey-type course in which we had sadly only a few days to spend on each author. I called it a "major figures" course so that I could focus on about a dozen writers in some depth, filling in with lesser writers at the rate of, sometimes, two or three per class

(Andrew Marvell in twenty minutes!). As a result, it was content-loaded with a lot of reading. While I didn't assign an unreasonable number of pages per class session, what I did assign was pretty challenging reading. (How many of my students actually read the assigned selections from *Paradise Lost*, for example, I will never know).

After this first class, which I spent primarily on reviewing the course requirements and the semester's assignment sheet, a student approached me with her version of the "I'm overwhelmed" speech. She was a tall, thin, kind of droopy girl with about a yard of straight blond hair, dark at her part, and a mouth full of braces. She had a pink back pack slung over one shoulder and rested her hand tipped with metallic green fingernails on my desk. She looked at me, then away, shrugged her shoulders and then said, I didn't know there would be reading. She used that whining tone students adopt to imply that somehow, in some way, the professor has betrayed them. And what, I asked in response, does the word "literature" mean to you--as in English Literature, the title of this course?--actually curious about what she would answer. Well, you know, she said, Cliff Notes for books, I guess. I stifled every sarcastic comment that came to mind and just smiled and said, I'm not a fan of Cliff Notes. Needless to say, this budding scholar did not return to the class. But surprisingly, the rest remained and the class stayed at seventeen students until the end of the term, one of my huge success stories.

When I returned to my office at 3:00 PM, there was a line of students waiting in the hall to see me about changing the composition course into which they had been placed as the result of placement tests taken before the term started. Authorizing placement changes was one of my administrative responsibilities. Some students were outraged that they had gotten a remedial placement (they were in honors English in high school!). Others were panicked about their college-entry placement, certain they didn't have the requisite skills. Others had been sent to me by various professors who wanted the student's placement checked. I knew I could not solve all their problems that afternoon, so ascertaining which kids could return the next morning and sending them away until then, I worked my way through those who were left and got most of them sorted out by 5:00 PM. This was the part of my job that took an enormous amount of time during the first week or ten days of the semester, but one that had to be done to insure that students were not wasting their time in a class that was either too simple or too demanding for their skills. Placement tests are good, but they're not perfect and students require a course that meets their needs.

I was tired by 5:00 PM. I always found that at the start of each term I was exhausted during the first week or so, especially in the fall after my long, relaxed summer. When the last student left, I went down to the faculty lounge and got some stale, lukewarm coffee from the communal pot. I dumped what was left of the coffee into the sink, washed out the pot, made a new pot for the evening faculty, and went back to my office to relax for a minute, get a little caffeine boost, and then leave for home, dinner, and early to bed.

Just as I was about to lock my office door and get away, my office phone rang. I debated whether or not to answer it, but then went back into my office, put my purse and briefcase on the desk and picked up the phone. It was Christie on the phone, alternately screeching and babbling, and it actually took me a while to recognize who this out-of-context caller was. When she calmed down and her voice clicked in as recognizable, I heard her telling me that Jimmy was in a 72-hour hold in a psychiatric ward in a Washington D. C. hospital, pending criminal investigation. I stood there listening, certain I was hearing my fragile little divorce collapse once again, my peace caving in on me.

I told Christie I'd call her back as soon as I got home, in thirty minutes or less, and then I hung up and left. The phone started to ring again as I was halfway down the hall to the stairs, but this time I let it ring. I was gone for the day.

CHAPTER 18

The drive home was awful. For some reason traffic was more sluggish than usual, I seemed to lose every traffic light between the college and home, and inexplicably at this time of day, the bridge over the river was up, causing a huge traffic backup and an additional twenty minute delay. I sat amidst the bridge traffic for what seemed like an eternity, waiting for the drawbridge to slowly work its way back down, the bridge man (or whatever they called him) to slowly push back the gates, the flashing lights to go off and the traffic light finally to change back to green. My inner agitation seemed to put everything into slow motion during which time I kept rehearsing Christie's call. What the hell was Jimmy doing in Washington in the first place? What crazy thing had he done to inspire a criminal investigation? Surely, he had not had enough time to pick up yet another lady friend, court her, lose her, and then stalk her. He had seemed to have learned his lesson so clearly from the Canada affair that I simply couldn't believe he'd repeat that folly.

I finally got home and before calling Christie back, poured two fingers of vodka into a glass with some ice, a drink which I intended to sip from as we spoke, for all the obvious reasons. I dialed, and as the phone rang in Christie's apartment and I stood in my kitchen waiting for her to answer, I opened my freezer and selected a frozen dinner--meat loaf and mashed potatoes, comfort food imbued with enough monosodium glutamate to poison several mice. I also pulled a head of lettuce from the crisper in the fridge with some vague notion of adding a salad to my TV dinner for health reasons. I don't think too well when it comes to constructing a healthy diet at the best of times, and this was not the best of times. On the fifth ring, Christie picked up, her voice this time sounding low and zombie-like. I sipped my vodka as she made her way through the baroque tale of Jimmy's adventure in Washington. From what I could piece together from her once-again choppy narrative, he had started out his day by shopping for a new car, a Mercedes-Benz, at a local dealership in New Jersey and had arranged to take one of the vehicles on a test drive. Instead of taking the normal neighborhood drive, he inexplicably drove the car to our nation's capitol, technically car theft, I guess. The panicked car salesman reported the car stolen after Jimmy did not return after three hours. Meanwhile, arriving in D. C., Jimmy looked up an old friend of his who was serving in the House of Representatives and convinced his friend that he had a matter of national security that he absolutely had to share with Janet Reno, the then Attorney General. He must have sounded reasonably sane because his friend, the congressman, was able to arrange a meet between Jimmy and some member of Janet Reno's staff. What happened after that is not clear; Jimmy had some paranoid story about how Merrill Lynch (the giant investment company) was planning to overthrow the United States government, apparently citing some patently insane evidence for this alleged plot (involving secret codes embedded in the Dow Jones). When

Reno's staff member tried to politely disengage with Jimmy, Jimmy apparently became disruptive. A security member who was asked to escort him to his car, as a matter of course checked the plates (which were suspicious because they were dealer plates), and subsequently discovered the stolen car report. I guess an arrest followed and then more bizarre behavior on Jimmy's part ensued which landed him in the psych ward at Georgetown University Hospital on a three-day hold to try to determine his mental state.

Throughout this lengthy narrative, I had time to pour another shot of vodka into my glass, but I just couldn't seem to find the right questions to ask. I couldn't ask what triggered Jimmy's odyssey. I couldn't ask if Christie had seen him recently. I couldn't even ask what was being done, but Christie did offer that as soon as she had been contacted (by the hospital staff person who got her information from Jimmy's wallet) she had called John, who had alerted a lawyer he knew in DC and was driving down there himself. Poor John. Bailing Jimmy out was becoming his default occupation. Meanwhile, they were trying out all sorts of anti-psychotic drugs on Jimmy and trying to formulate some kind of diagnosis. Because he appeared to be seriously delusional, schizophrenia was the hot choice.

Don't go down there, I said to Christie. Just don't go. This is one drama you don't want to be a part of. She was crying by now and saying, over and over, he really *is* crazy. Look, I said, if it helps, think that way, that he is sick. Mental illness is not his fault, nor is much of the related behavior. And the good news is that maybe now, finally, he will be able to get some real help. They have some good drugs for this, and therapy, I don't know. But they are not going to just let him walk back out into the world and keep this up.

But, in fact, unless the diagnosis after the 72-hour hold suggested that he was a danger either to himself or to others, that's exactly what they were going to do--let him out of the hospital with some pills and then probably return him to New Jersey and arrest him for car theft, unless Janet Reno's office wanted to press some kind of federal charges for disorderly conduct (assuming that they don't get nuts like Jimmy every day in their offices). However it worked out, to keep him any longer in a psychiatric facility would require his consent for transfer and commitment to a longer-term stay, something which I knew he would never do. I didn't specify this to Christie, but I felt that somehow I had to get in touch with John and have that "conversation," the one that both of us, especially John, had been avoiding since my separation from Jimmy had started. The man was sick, needed help, and needed it now.

Christie didn't know where John would be staying in DC, and so after my call with Christie ended, I called John's home and spoke with his wife. She didn't know where he'd be staying either, because he had left for D.C. in a terrific hurry, but she promised to give him the message to call me as soon as he contacted her to tell her where he was. I impressed on her the urgency of this call and she said, of course, of course, in a tone that communicated to me that she understood everything, or at least understood that this was a crisis of a very special nature.

I had this very vague but panicked notion that, as the wife of record, someone from Georgetown University Hospital or Janet Reno's office or the New Jersey Mercedes dealership might be contacting me for something or other, that I might somehow find myself responsible for making choices about my ersatz husband's status, choices that I in no way wanted to be making. I couldn't even wrap my head around the possibility that perhaps crazy people could not consent to a legal divorce. I was too afraid to contact Gabe and get his legal advice on this. Not just yet. Let's see what miracles John or the D.C. lawyer could work and maybe with a little luck, I wouldn't have to tell Gabe anything or do anything or even think anything. Maybe six weeks would just pass, Jimmy would come to court on October 17, agree to everything everyone said, and it would be over, over, over.

I'm not sure how I survived the next few hours. I put the vodka bottle away, made my pathetic meat loaf and salad dinner, ate very little of it, watched the news on TV, half expecting to hear about a nut-case arrested in Janet Reno's offices (I didn't), and finally, finally, got into my pajamas and bathrobe, turned down my bed, and prepared to stare at the wall until John called, or until I fell asleep, whichever came first. Neither came first. What--or, more specifically, who--came first was Christie. My doorbell rang about nine-thirty and there on my doorstep, looking pale and disheveled, was Christie with a small duffel slung over her shoulder, dressed in jeans and a pink t-shirt, looking all of about eighteen years old. My God, I said, come in. How did you get here? Train, she answered, and then a taxi from the train station. She walked in, went straight to the guest room, "her room," where she dumped her duffel, and then came to join me in the kitchen. So out came the vodka bottle again and while I didn't join her, poured her a stiff one. After we both ascertained that neither of us had heard from John and so had no updates, we launched on a long, rambling conversation about all the possible ramifications of the current situation--which eventually led to past situations, and finally, at least for me, to exhaustion. Look, I said, I absolutely have to go to work tomorrow, no way can I take off the second day of the semester. So, I'm going to bed. Sleep as long as you want, I told her, take whatever food you can find. I'll call here from work tomorrow about 1:00 PM or you call me there if you hear anything from John or from anyone. I'll try to get home by five or five-thirty. That's just what I have to do. Sounds good, Christie muttered sleepily. I just had to come, she said. I knew I would never sleep if I didn't come. No, no, I said, it's OK. I get it. I'm glad you came. I just have to go to bed. And I did.

The next day I had the expected lineup of students, waiting for me outside my office when I arrived at 8:00 AM, and then I had two classes in a row to teach, at 9:30 and 11:00. If I got a call from Christie that morning, I never knew it as there were no messages from her when I checked in at my office, so I called her at my house when I got back to my office about 12:30. I had more students to see and then a meeting at 2:00 PM, so I was hoping there would be no news, nothing to discuss, nothing to cheer Christie up about. The phone rang and rang in my house until it went to the answering machine. I left a message for Christie in case she was there and just not picking up or in case she'd check my messages before I got home. I wondered where she was, lacking a car or any known associates in the area, but I had long ago learned never to expect predictable behavior from Christie and not to get unduly worried about her. In fact, I quickly forgot about her, my mind elsewhere as I met with students continuously until 2:00 PM and then dashed off to my meeting. It was a tedious department meeting with all the boring start-of-term announcements that seldom varied from semester to semester but had to be delivered nonetheless. Our Dean held a full department meeting to begin with and then split the English faculty off from the rest and I met with the English types while he met with the others, both of us reviewing what in my profession were called "discipline specific" matters. Because English types like to talk, and love to debate, my part of the meeting went on after the other concurrent meeting finished, well past 3:30, until someone suggested we table a few contentious matters and we were able to adjourn.

When I got back to my office, I had a few in-office phone messages to return and several items in my mail that required my attention or my signature right then and when I finished, it was past 4:30. Rather than try Christie again, I decided just to leave. Whatever was going on, it surely could wait half an hour until I got home. I always worked very hard to separate my life at home--good, bad or indifferent-- from my life at work. To me, they were two totally different spheres, each working best when it did not intrude on the other. It was a compartmentalization that had worked well for me for more than twenty-five years, enhanced by my geographical distance from the campus. Although I liked many of my colleagues from school, we rarely socialized--apart from occasional faculty parties or during out of town conferences--nor did my friends from home know anyone with whom I worked. It might appear that I had things in each sphere to hide from people in the other, but that wasn't true. I just thought of them as two separate and relatively incompatible worlds. What I did in one, I hardly ever did in the other. Occasionally, I would wonder if I'd actually like working with someone I knew socially or if I'd actually like playing golf or partying with someone from the college. With very few exceptions over the years, I never had to find out. My friends at home thought the only "real" doctors were MDs and my colleagues from school thought that golf was the way dilettantes wasted four hours.

So, as I drove home that day, the traffic was mercifully light, and I crossed the bridge over that river that separated the county in which I worked from the county in which I lived. I crossed that bridge every day, five days a week, once going and once coming home and it was a real bridge, steel and concrete, now dazzlingly white in the late afternoon sun, American flags flying straight out in a stiff west wind, a few sea gulls perched on its railings; but it was also part of my symbolic geography. As I drove over it, I took a deep breath and knew I was leaving student and curricular and teaching and learning matters behind and going home to discover how the indescribable events of Jimmy's shattered life would continue to spread it's long fingers into mine and into the lives of others. I was thinking of those lines from *The Great Gatsby* where Nick Caraway describes Daisy and Tom Buchanan as careless people who made messes and then left other people to clean up after them, and I was getting both angry and sick of Jimmy and his messes. I was tired of the entanglements of the incredibly unnecessary dramas created by the sick mind and woefully shattered ego that constituted Jimmy, that awful, sad, tedious and boring, yes, boring Jimmy. Enough. Never boring? I don't think so. There is nothing more boring than redundant crises of which you wanted no part, crises that had no meaning except to a broken man who had no identity other than as the creator of dramas. I knew in some vague way that he was terribly sick. OK. But at that moment, I just didn't care.

When I got home, there was a note from Christie on the kitchen counter. She had gotten restless, had called an "old friend," and he was going to pick her up, take her to lunch and then to the train. She was going back to the city, was bored with this whole new Daddy thing. Fuck it, she noted. She'd call me later. John had called and she left his contact number. Whatever Christie did, whatever she was thinking, I couldn't fault it. Hadn't I just driven over my bridge thinking how angry and bored I was by it all, too? I debated as to whether or not I would call John, after all, whether I would pursue my panic-driven need to keep Jimmy whole for just a few more months until I could legally be free of him forever. Or whether, like Christie, I would just say fuck it.

I turned on the TV and watched the local nightly news, not really seeing or hearing any of it. I debated ordering a pizza but then just pulled out another of my inevitable frozen dinners, put it in the microwave, and poured myself a glass of wine. I ate about half the dinner, and poured the unfinished glass of wine down the sink. The decision I finally made was cowardly, but I made it anyway: I would call John and then, depending upon what he told me, would contact my lawyer and let him be my advocate from here on out. I'm out of it. Contact my lawyer. That's what my new mantra would be. See you in court. Whatever.

I finally spoke with John later that evening after two earlier unsuccessful attempts to reach him at his hotel in Washington. By the time I spoke with him, he'd visited with Jimmy, who was sedated and relatively useless when it came to a factual accounting of what had happened. John and the D.C. lawyer he had engaged went out and back-tracked Jimmy's day in the nation's capital to Janet Reno's office and discovered there would be no issues there. Jimmy's conduct had been rude and disruptive, but no criminal charges would be filed. He had been detained mainly when the car theft charges emerged and then hospitalized due to a major irrational and delusional melt down at the police station. John had then been in touch with the Mercedes dealer by telephone, assuring him that the car, while impounded by the D. C. police, was unharmed and would be returned to him in any manner he deemed acceptable as soon as possible with appropriate damages paid--for loss of use, transport, pain and suffering, whatever else they felt was appropriate. The dealer was still quite angry, but John seemed to think they could work something out whereby legal charges would be dropped in recognition that Jimmy was currently in a psychiatric facility and was not in his "right mind" when he took the car to D. C. as well as the apology money, thrown in as a big sweetener or bribe, depending on your point of view.

On the legal side, John said he would attempt to get Jimmy to consent to remain in the psychiatric facility until a diagnosis was made, perhaps for an additional week, and then to have him released to John's custody with further arrangements for psychiatric care and medication back in New Jersey. I had the good grace not to mention Jimmy's "fitness" for divorce to John, who sounded weary and deflated beyond belief. My divorce was not his problem. At one point, John said, I just don't know how much more of this I can do. I told him I thought that with counseling and medication--and perhaps a move to Florida--that Jimmy would improve and cease to be a burden. At least, I prayed that could be. John said, so do I, so do I.

I didn't call Gabe that night. It was too late. I decided that this issue required a face-to-face visit and so would call his office in the morning and try to make a late-afternoon appointment with him as soon as was possible. That was all I had the energy for that night. I walked into my bedroom, fell onto my bed, and went immediately to sleep, waking some time after midnight. I staggered around the house, turning off lights, and then got undressed and got properly into bed, remembering to turn on the alarm clock, and I slept until it went off at six the next morning. I slept without any dreams at all, or, again, any that I could recall.

CHAPTER 19

Remarkably, everything ended more or less the way John had hoped and planned it would. Jimmy was eventually diagnosed after testing and examination during an extended stay in the hospital, and the court agreed to extradition to New Jersey and the New Jersey court, in turn, agreed to his probationary release into John's custody, the probationary continuance reliant upon Jimmy's compliance with the court stipulation that he get counseling and stay on the prescribed medications. The psychiatric diagnosis was a kind of complex version of bipolar disorder with something delusional embedded in the findings. I neither sought nor obtained the details. John found him a psychiatrist, helped put his condo up for sale, and worked with a realtor in Florida, long distance, finding Jimmy a condo there, close to John's new winter home, a condo that Jimmy actually liked and that was available for purchase and occupancy on January 1.

After his return from D.C., Jimmy went more or less to ground, sticking close to home, seeing his shrink and reporting to his probation officer as required. He met John for lunch on occasion but did not go near his club and spoke to John about resigning. He was required to take blood tests to ascertain that he stayed on his meds and off alcohol. On both counts, he complied. There was some uncertainty as to when he would be allowed to move to Florida, but John said it didn't matter when he'd get the release. The condo would be his and if he sold his condo in New Jersey and still couldn't move, he could stay at John's house until he was allowed to go to Florida.

At my face-to-face meeting with Gabe where I gave him all the details I had at the time, his advice was more or less to sit tight (something I was getting good at, having done so for more than a year). The idea was that if Jimmy appeared for the court date, the decree would be granted. Whatever else Gabe had to do, if anything, to ensure that the decree would in fact be legitimate and would be granted, he never mentioned.

And so October 17 finally, finally came and that morning at 9:00 AM, Gabe picked me up at home and we drove together to the courthouse. It was a pretty fall day, sunny and cool. The world looked scrubbed and clean, the trees tinted for the season. Gabe looked handsome and business-like, very impressive in his grey pinstripe suit and rep tie, his slightly graying hair adding just the right touch of gravitas; I wore a black pants suit, the one I saved for funerals. I was unexpectedly calm when we got there, repressing all worst case scenarios and just walking the endless miles of halls in the courthouse alongside Gabe to the appointed room. There was one case ahead of us, an incredibly young-looking black couple with a small child, a little girl who looked to be about three, clinging to her mother's leg. This couple went into the small courtroom and were in there for an inexplicably long time, and then reappeared, the little girl now asleep, positioned over her mother's shoulder like a sack of something soft and pink. As we were waiting, Jimmy came down the hall, alone. He approached us, shook hands with Gabe, and gave me a light kiss on the cheek, and then took a seat in a wooden chair across the corridor from us. As always, after seeing him after a long absence, my heart started to beat a little irregularly. I took deep breaths. He looked pale and thinner, but well dressed in a navy blue suit. He disliked navy blue suits, I knew, but I was too distracted to care or wonder why he chose to wear this one today. I didn't want to think any personal thoughts about him, to remember things, to know things about him that only love would tell. I was happy and in some odd way amazed that he had shown up, even though Gabe had assured me that he was going to, and I wanted no other emotions to surface. I knew my calm was fragile, like thin oil spread on the ocean's surface, and I didn't want to disturb it.

After the young couple, their lawyers, and their sleeping child had wandered away down the hall, we were called into the small, non-descript courtroom. Our hearing was short and to the point. We answered the judge's questions as briefly as possible. Jimmy indicated that he was *pro se* for the proceedings and the judge did not object. After what seemed like just the blink of an eye, it was over, we signed the necessary papers, and the decree was granted. We stepped back out into the hall and Jimmy shook hands again with Gabe--and this time, shook my hand, too. He asked in a soft, low-pitched voice, without much enthusiasm, if we'd like to go for lunch, but both Gabe and I demurred, politely, pleading previous engagements, and so Jimmy turned and walked off. I watched his figure recede back down the hall, a tall, distinguished, and attractive man by any external measure, and then I watched him disappear around a corner and I thought, good-bye Jimmy. Good-bye.

Part Three:
Aftermath

The art of losing isn't hard to master;
so many things seem filled with the intent
to be lost that their loss is no disaster.

Elizabeth Bishop, "One Art"

CHAPTER 20

I once wrote a poem about Jimmy which I titled: *To My Ex-Husband, with Love*. It began:

I love everyone that I have ever loved
So why not you? With all the arrogance
Still on your pretty face, I do.

I wrote this after returning from a trip to Florida about four years after our divorce. I had rented a condo for the month of January in West Palm Beach, but upon his invitation, had driven up to Jimmy's condo in Vero Beach, ostensibly to "see it," but also to see him, to walk with him on the beach, to drive around and see all his haunts, to dine out at a big restaurant on the water, and, yes, to stay over night (in the guest room) and then leave the next day. There was no sex, no romance; by that time we'd established the new rules of engagement. We were, as Jimmy liked to say with mild sarcasm, *just* friends.

I liked his new house in Vero Beach. It was a stucco bungalow with a small gated front yard, lush with plantings; it had a spacious foyer, a small eat-in kitchen, a large dining room and living room, two bedrooms and two baths, and a charming little glassed-in sun porch in back, off the living room, looking out onto a walled-in garden with a little fountain ensconced in one of the walls, trickling out water and playing with the light. This back garden was, as in the front, lush with the semi tropical growth so typical of southern Florida, bright red, orange and yellow flowers and a small lime tree in one corner. Oh, this is so nice, I said. I'm so happy that you have such a nice place to live. It was, of course, one detached cottage among many that were identical, but this was a redundancy that could be overlooked once inside. Jimmy had used much of his former furniture (some of it from "our" house) as well as prints and paintings from the apartment to furnish the place and it looked quite settled and homey and even a touch elegant.

I had seen him since the divorce, but never in Florida, never at his home and I felt unusually pleased that he had, in Christie's words, landed on his feet once again. Really, he was nothing if not a survivor, maddening and admirable all at once. He seemed to me to be relatively calm during that visit and I suspected he was "on" his meds at that point. There were times before--and would be times after--that we, John and I, suspected (or knew) that he had abandoned the pharmaceutically induced calm for episodes of pill-free lunacy. I could even sense it in the phone calls which were our major source of contact after the divorce. When I heard that manic tone in his voice, filled with frenetic energy, describing high-blown plans and adventures, I was always more than suspicious that he was off the meds and on the manic track. But then, I was fifteen hundred miles away. Even so, I did what I could and never avoided our telephone conversations.

I don't specifically remember how or why we regained contact after our D-day in the courthouse, but it is important for me to chronicle the relationship that followed--our "friendship"--as best as I can in order to remember our story in its entirety, because it did not, as expected, end after the divorce.

I think Jimmy must have called me, initially, weeks or months after the divorce. I think the occasion was to tell me of his plans to move to Florida, full time, as he previously had discussed with John soon after the Washington, D. C. debacle. He had, in fact, put his New Jersey condo up for sale and put down interest money on the Florida place. I don't specifically remember the details of our conversation during that call, other than me being surprised to hear from him, but do know that I knew even before he made the actual move to Florida, that he was going, so he must have called me sometime in March or April. I recall playing in a guest day golf tournament with John's wife in the May after the divorce and remember that when she told me that Jimmy had moved to Florida, I was not surprised, that I already knew he had gone. From that first call forward, I always got the impression that Jimmy called because he wanted me to approve of what he was doing, wanted to show me that he was doing just fine, and wanted me to understand that his life was going on swimmingly without me. Knowing all that didn't really matter to me, though, because I liked talking to him regardless.

His calls were not frequent, every few months or so, but I never found them unwelcome. He always called at times that were convenient and we usually had long talks that covered a wide range of subjects. Jimmy continued to be smart, witty, and seemed, with some odd exceptions, to have worked out a reasonably good life for himself. He saw John during the winter months and seemed to have discovered some old friends--Jimmy was never short of old friends-- now retired in the area where he had settled. When I would remark to one friend of mine or another, on occasion, that I had talked to my ex-husband recently on the phone, I invariably got odd looks or weird chuckles in response--and, of course, from Lee I got the continuing refrain that over is *over*, not your problem. Notwithstanding, when he called, I always said, hi Jimmy, and talked with him, sometimes for as much as an hour. I never called him, but that didn't seem to bother him or change his pattern of calling me. He never called at odd hours--too early or too late--and never alluded to anything provocative concerning our former life together or the events that had ended it. He was always very interested in what was going on with Bella and, I think, called her a few times, too. I don't recall Bella being upset with these calls either--or, at least, she never said so. Jimmy was just sort of there in our lives, a force of nature, the ghost in the machine, the unicorn in the garden, the friendly shadow. Our ex.

The first time I actually saw him following the divorce came shortly after I sold the house, as I had vaguely planned to do on that pre-divorce day lying on my bed, taking stock of my future. I sold it in the summer following our divorce and purchased a new one in the same town, really only a few blocks away. I was still living in "our" former house, however, scene of the crimes, waiting to have the new place painted and carpeted before moving in. Jimmy had come up north on business concerning some properties he owned in New York and had suggested we meet for lunch while he was "in town." I agreed, not even feeling very dramatic about this, and before we went for lunch, I stopped to show him my new house. It was a house I truly loved, filled with light, with a little view of the river across the street, surrounded by woods and gardens on a small lane that ran between two quiet streets. It had the charm that the other house could never have. The rooms were small, but there were nine of them--I had had an office built off the breakfast room so I could retain all three bedrooms--mine, and then one for Bella and the third one for guests--and still have an office. I always wanted Bella to have her own room in my house, regardless, and not just a room that was my office or my guest room. I wanted her always to have a room of her own so that it was her home for however long she was there.

In addition to the standard living room, dining room, kitchen, three bedrooms, and two baths, the house also had a charming breakfast room that opened onto a small deck, as well as a sunroom off my bedroom that opened on to a larger deck. Jimmy liked the house. He said it was perfect for me, lovely, and I knew this was not sarcasm or even a reference to the Queen Bee syndrome of which I had been formerly accused. I was unusually pleased by his comments.

Another small event I recall from that visit was that when Jimmy came to pick me up for lunch, before we toured my new home, I introduced him to my new puppy. My dear old cat had finally passed away at the age of 21 and so I had purchased a little Westie puppy in the spring. As I was talking to the dog before we left for lunch, petting his nose and reminding him to be a good boy while we were gone, Jimmy remarked, only half in jest, that I was nicer to the dog than I had ever been to him. I didn't say a word but thought then and still think now that perhaps he was right, metaphorically at least.

My final memory from that visit was from lunch. We had decided to sit at the bar, have a drink, order, and then go into the dining room to eat. While we were sitting there waiting for our drinks, for whatever reason, Jimmy started telling me about his current sex life, in details that were not totally graphic, but specific enough to embarrass me--especially since Jimmy was using a conversational tone that I was certain the bartender could hear and was in fact listening to every word. I said something like I don't really need to know this, trying to signal to Jimmy that the bartender was listening, but Jimmy was perversely ignoring me until I said, pointedly--I don't think the whole bar needs to know this either, at which point he looked around, a little confused, and then stopped his narrative. He later apologized to me, laughing a little, saying he guessed he just got carried away. I privately thought the whole thing was totally purposeful on his part--but I never said. The rest of the meal was pleasant, as was a reunion that could have been a whole lot worse.

CHAPTER 21

Also after the divorce, I began renting a condo in Florida for the month of January. Intersession break for faculty at the college ran from right before Christmas to the last week in January, so it was a great time to get away and recharge. Often, I was able to gain access to my rental in Florida a few days before the first of January so that I could leave home right after Christmas. Sometimes I drove down with a friend who was going for the season; sometimes I flew down. Either way, I rented a car when I got there. I always had to leave Florida about the 20th of January to get back in time for the start of the second semester, so I always paid for more time in the condo than I spent there--but it was worth it. During these January trips south, Bella or one or another of my friends from home would often come down and spend time with me, so I always rented a two-bedroom apartment in order to accommodate my visitors. After a few years in various locations, I settled on one particular place in a gated community in West Palm Beach, a large settlement of homes, condos and apartments with a lovely club house and golf course on the grounds. The apartment I rented was on the second (top) floor of a four-apartment unit, overlooking one of the winding waterways that flowed through the community. It was a pretty setting, very private and peaceful, all the apartment units surrounded by enough foliage to mask their proximity, and even when I was there by myself, I was never lonely and enjoyed a perfect refuge from my life "up north." I actually never saw one neighbor from the other three apartments the whole time I was there over several Januarys. I had many friends who wintered in that area of Florida, so lunches, dinners and golf games were generally available for me.

There was a pool a short walk down from my apartment and on my way there one day I made one of the few new friends I ever made in Florida. Walking down to the pool alone, late on a sunny morning, I was joined by a young man carrying a home-made fishing pole who introduced himself as Joseph. Hi, I'm Joseph, who are you, he said with great candor. He was clearly a Downs Syndrome person, very chatty and friendly, telling me all about his fishing expedition, presumably on the bank of the waterway that ran through the community, which had, to my knowledge, no fish. Nonetheless, as we walked, I listened with pleasure to Joseph's depiction of his planned fishing expedition, including a lunch break with a peanut butter sandwich that he had brought along and showed me with pride. We parted ways as I reached the pool and I wished him a good catch. Later in the week, I saw him at the pool with a man whom I assumed to be his father. The young man recognized me and came over to talk. His father started to restrain him but I said, oh no, we're buddies, right Joseph? Throughout that vacation, I had regular chats with Joseph, one of the nicest people I have ever met. I occasionally asked him if he had caught any fish and he invariably answered, no, but I will tomorrow. That's how Joseph looked at life.

One January in the mid-nineties, a few years after I had made that trip to Vero Beach to visit Jimmy at his Florida home, I had a call from him at my rental. He said he was planning to be in West Palm for a few days the following week and would call me when he got into town so we could maybe have dinner or something. I told him on what dates I was free for the following week and those apparently fit his plans, so we left it that he'd call when he got to town on Wednesday. He explained only that he would be visiting someone in the area.

In fact, he called me back on the next Tuesday morning, a day earlier than expected, as I was on my way out to meet friends for a golf game. He asked if we could have a late supper that night and I said OK, gave him directions to my apartment, and hung up. Then I called the guard at the entry gate to let him know I was expecting a guest that evening, specifying name and approximate arrival time. I had been planning, until he called, to go over to a nearby dining spot owned by friends of mine that evening--just pop in for a drink and an app at the bar and have some chit-chat with the wife of the owner--but since I hadn't notified my friends of this intent and thus had nothing to really cancel, figured I could go the next night or the next. Jimmy had sounded, if not urgent, anxious. I wondered what was up. (Something was always up with him, wasn't it?)

After a nice golf game with friends and a late lunch, I drove back to my apartment at about 3:30 PM that Tuesday, engaged by the ever-shifting scenes along the highway--1A1a or whatever its name, I always lost track of the reductionist number-letter labeling of this road. There were luxurious strip malls, set back amidst lush tropical greenery and palms; then there would be a garish auto repair storefront with garage bay doors open to reveal cars in various states of disassembly set next to a MacDonald's alongside an ornate church. Florida's ideas about zoning were slim to none. Apparently, whoever bought the land could erect whatever structures they wanted with almost no restrictions or building codes that the eye could see. The result was this carnival mish-mash of shops, businesses, and restaurants-- every so often a motel or a church--sporting designs from the ultra chic to the outright bizarre. On my own corner, where I turned west to get to the huge sprawling compound that housed my rental, there was a gigantic shopping mall on the northeast corner, with dozens of stores as well as a movie multiplex boasting fifteen theaters. On the southeast corner there was an International House of Pancakes. The remaining corners had a huge self-serve gas station and car wash and a luxe furniture store, respectively. About a mile down this road was the entrance to Howard's End, the odd name given to my "gated community." I doubted that its developers had either read E. M. Forrester or watched Merchant-Ivory films, so I amused myself imagining the odd circumstances that might have given rise to the naming of the complex.

It was all very pretty. The entrance was heavily landscaped around the elaborate white stucco gatehouse structure that spanned the four lane divided entry road, a gatehouse that barred all but the residents and their guests from entry. Once through the entrance gates, the cobblestone streets of the community wound their way around lovely homes, some quite large, waterways, little ornate bridges crossing the canals, and then continuing alongside parts of the golf course, past flowered parks, past the entrance drive to the main clubhouse, and then past various markers signaling entrances to the condo or apartment sections of the community. The entrance to my area was marked by two white brick columns on either side of the road with insert plaques announcing "Waterway," the name of my section. Although apparently arbitrary and natural, casual and rambling, the entire place was really very well-planned and orderly, easy to navigate and easy on the eye. The terrain was almost totally flat and so was attractive for walking, even for those who did not really like to walk (like me). I walked for what I think now was more than a mile most mornings, almost without noticing that I was actually exercising. There was usually a light dew and a nice breeze, always cool enough to enjoy the mild morning.

So, I got home that day from my golf game and lunch, lay on the chaise in the screened-in porch with a book and relaxed for a while. I may have dozed off, but finally roused myself about 6:00 PM, took a shower, dressed and waited for Jimmy, who showed up a little before eight. He apologized again for the late arrival, even though he had cautioned me about it on the phone; and then he went on to say, but visiting hours are over at 7:30. I know I was supposed to ask who he was visiting and the old rules about not taking the bait didn't apply in this situation, really, but I didn't ask anyway. Jimmy said he'd tell me the whole story at dinner, so I didn't really need to ask. I had a feeling the visiting hours were going to be all about his presence in Palm Beach and that there was probably a woman starring in this drama and, as it turned out, on both counts I was right.

We left my apartment, got into Jimmy's latest version of his series of ubiquitous white Cadillacs and drove back around the cobblestone roads and out of Howard's End, making our way to a popular local restaurant in Palm Beach, crowded, Italian, elegant, a little noisier than what one usually finds in Palm Beach, but we were seated in a relatively quiet corner. We ordered cocktails and Jimmy told his tale.

He was in love again. What a surprise. Melissa. What a name. I have to say that I thought it was somewhere between touching and psychotic that after all of his life's extraordinary romantic experiences, our own little chapter included, he could still believe in love--in that particular kind of love that usually happens before the age of twenty-five--not quite the naive puppy-love variety, but the this-might-last-forever variety, the kind of love that truly only happens in movies but that Jimmy kept seeking--and finding seemingly *ad infinitum*--if only for a few days, weeks or months. This time, the twist was that his new love, while appropriately blond, beautiful, and financially secure, was also older, about sixty, an alcoholic and a drug abuser. She was currently in a rehab center in Palm Beach and Jimmy was theoretically in town to visit her but, in fact, had come down to bust her out, in response to her frantic and repeated requests during numerous day and night phone calls. Now, however, after having actually seen her, he was uncertain that the escape plan was really advisable, and had put her off for a day. She was apparently in pretty bad shape with many unattractive withdrawal symptoms and Jimmy was actually asking me what I thought about the escape plan.

You're kidding, right, I said? I mean, you are actually asking me what I think about this *plan*? You have a carton of cigarettes and her warm-up suit in the back seat of your car and have this fucked up *plan* to wheel her out in a laundry basket or covered up on a gurney and you are asking me what I *think*? So, OK, I said, I'll tell you what I think. Unless she is in that place on a court order, which I doubt, she's free to leave any damn time she pleases which you damn well know as you have had, um, some experience along these lines. So don't give me *escape* and all the dramatic crap that goes with it. She could walk out of that place tonight, assuming she's paid up, and if you won't drive her home, she can call a cab. Which no doubt she *will* do if you don't go along with the *plan*. So what is it you are really asking me? What? You want my permission? You want me to know all about your latest drama? Why are you here at all--instead of on the road back to Vero Beach with a blond in a pale blue warm up suit smoking Kent cigarettes in the passenger seat of your car? I hadn't realized at the start of my diatribe how really angry all of this made me--this adolescent misunderstanding of life, this badly-told grade B movie drama, this misaligned self image of Jimmy as savior, hero, whatever. I was just so *sick* of it all. But I hadn't meant to get so angry.

Well, for all my sarcasm, I was nonetheless technically wrong, because it seems that I didn't have the whole story.

"She"--really, truly named Melissa--in fact *was* admitted to the detox center under some kind of legal order after all, because she'd been found face-down on a fur rug by her visiting son in her sunken living room in her large home in Vero Beach, unconscious, blotto drunk with a tox screen that would light up a movie marquee. Rushed to the hospital, she had apparently barely survived death from a variety of potential causes and, indeed, was being held in the Palm Beach facility (chosen by her son for its reputation and pizzazz) as a "danger to herself" and thus was not subject, at the moment, to self-decreed release. Nonetheless, she was calling Jimmy hourly, all day and night, begging him to come get her, to save her, which of course he truly relished.

He excused himself once during dinner to use the restaurant's pay phone to call Melissa (she needs to hear from me, he explained). After dinner, we left the Italian place and went to Au Bar for a nightcap. We wanted to see the place kind of as a joke because of all the press it got during the William Kennedy Smith trial and we thought we might bump into Teddy Kennedy--which we didn't. As one columnist had put it a few years back at the time of the trial, Au Bar is dull, but at least it's expensive. I had to agree, it was both--although moderately enlivened for me by the fact that Jimmy excused himself to make two more phone calls to Melissa. Won't she kind of catch on to where you are calling from by the background noise, I asked--because Au Bar was expensive and dull, but it wasn't quiet. No, no, he said, I told her where I am. She doesn't care. She just wants me to come back in the morning and get her out. And what, I said, once you do that, will you do with her? Chain her to a wall? I mean, she's a drunk. Drunks drink. If she drinks, she'll die--so what do you do about that?

He looked at me. He shrugged, slowly, elegantly. He had on a green and white checked gingham shirt, a green blazer, white pants, white Gucci loafers, his silver hair shining against his tan. He really did look like a star. He said he thought she could stay at his house for a while and that after she moved back to her place he could keep an eye on her, make her take her medication. God, Jimmy, I said. It will take a lot more than eyes on and a few pills. I mean, I'm not even going to ask you why you want to take on this world of hurt (I get it, you love her), but could you at least admit that you have zero expertise in detoxification skills and that if you take her out of that place and she dies, you might just get yourself involved with a charge of manslaughter or reckless endangerment or some such? I mean, this is serious shit. She needs professional care. If you really love her, don't you want what's best for her rather than indulging some lunatic escape fantasy? I don't even know the woman and I know she needs professional help.

We talked like this for another half hour or so and then I just got bored with the entire episode. I was lighting cigarettes and stubbing them out half smoked in the big, square Au Bar ashtray. I was swirling my brandy in its snifter but not drinking it. Jimmy asked for advice but he didn't even hear it let alone consider taking any of it. I didn't know what the hell I was even doing there--except to serve as some sort of perverse audience for Jimmy's latest performance. Just as rich people needed guests, dramatic people needed an audience. But suddenly the show wasn't worth watching. Take her, I said. It's wrong and it's nuts and my advice is go back to Vero Beach alone, but take her because that's the way you've both written the script. I just hope to hell you both live through it. And just be aware that she may have a different ending in mind, Jimmy, very different. But Jimmy hated it when I talked in metaphors.

So we left our drinks unfinished on the table at dull expensive Au Bar and he drove me home; we bid each other a kind of curt good-night and I didn't hear from him again for months--and when I did, the call was to tell me that Melissa had died and that he was coming north for her funeral, but that he wasn't going to stop and see me. He had to spend all his time with her grieving family. So I assume you're not responsible for her death, more or less, I asked? No, he said. She slit her wrists. I left her in rehab after all, and then she was making progress, getting out for day trips. She was doing really well and was due to come home and then she just went into the ladies room at Ta-boo, you know, that little place on Worth Avenue in Palm Beach, and slit her wrists on a beautiful April day. She had been having lobster salad for lunch with her son.

And keep in mind, I never knew and never found out if Melissa, in all her glory and tragedy and beauty and blondness and junk, had ever even existed. All I ever saw of her was a pale blue warm-up suit and a carton of Kents in the back seat of Jimmy's car. But for whatever reason, I believed every word he said about her and I still do. As I said, he didn't get metaphor and he *really* didn't get symbols or dream wishes.

CHAPTER 22

And, contrary to common opinion, Jimmy was not a liar, if you discount lying by omission. I mentioned earlier that I didn't think he had had affairs with other women during the time we were married, but I never asked him. He could have. So, if he was unfaithful, he lied (of course) by omission. But what sane man in America says to his wife--oh, honey, by the way, I'm sleeping with my secretary for a while, but it doesn't really mean anything to me beyond sexual and ego gratification. No problem, right? Statistics suggest that more than 68% of married men cheat on their wives multiple times during the course of their marriages, so that would probably make 68% of married men liars by omission. But generally, Jimmy did not invent things or say things that were contrary to the facts or to the truth as he knew it, and if you asked him a direct question that he didn't want to answer, he might have some version of a temper tantrum to avoid response; but he really didn't lie much more than most people do, which is, I think, occasionally and mostly for good reason.

Because his life was so incredibly picaresque, it would be easy to think the stories he told were invented because they couldn't possibly be true--or at least, not so many of them could all belong to one person's life. But Jimmy did

not narrate even one-tenth of his life adventures to people-
-persons--friends. I probably knew a lot more because we
were together sharing stories for a long time and what I
didn't share in or what he didn't tell me, other people felt
moved to relate (often to persuade me what an incorrigible
rat he was). I believed the stories Jimmy told on himself a
lot more than I believed those told about him, stories which
had a tendency to take on fantastic overtones of the urban
legend variety in the re-telling.

Here is a brief example. Jimmy was a good golfer, very
good, and one year when he was fairly young--maybe forty-
-he was playing in the final round of his club championship.
He and his opponent reached the 36th tee all square, so
this hole would decide the winner or send the match to a
"sudden death" playoff. It was a par-3 and Jimmy hit a nice
drive to the center of the green, about 30 feel from the hole.
His opponent missed the green but chipped up to about six
feet from the hole. Jimmy's putt, his second shot, rolled to
about a foot from the hole and his opponent said "pick it
up," which meant he was conceding the putt and almost
conceding the match; so Jimmy picked up his ball which
is part of golf etiquette and also common sense (because
you could miss it). When a putt is given in match play, you
take it. And there is no rule prohibiting this in match play.
The opponent went on to miss his own putt and as Jimmy
was walking off the green as the victor, his opponent said
that Jimmy had forfeited the hole because he didn't putt
out. Jimmy just looked at him, walked off the course, and
never looked back. He lost the championship because he
could never prove that the other guy had cheated when he

denied that he had "given" Jimmy the putt. Apparently, the only other person who had heard him say "pick it up" was the opponent's caddie--and no caddie will ever bear witness against his player. So--stupid Jimmy for not putting out? Who knows.

But this story turned into one of the golf club's most exaggerated urban legends of all time. I heard versions that included vile threats, drunken insults, fisticuffs, law suits, vandalism--all on Jimmy's part--none of which ever happened. When I asked Jimmy why he didn't at least stick around and challenge the "gimme" putt, he just said, only three of us knew what really happened and two were going to lie. Why bother? Golf is either a game of honor or it isn't. He never played in the club championship again after that, although he probably had more than one chance to win. I don't know what I would have done under the circumstances and I don't know whether what Jimmy did do was stupid bravado or honorable adherence to the code--but I do know the story was exaggerated out of all proportion except when it was told by Jimmy (his version confirmed by a few truthful witnesses). His version never changed, and I believed it. So maybe there were some ugly truths he never told; but I think what he did tell was pretty accurate. And I know he never cheated in golf, at least not when I was there.

On the other hand, lest he sound like a saint, he once told me a rather nasty little tale about a man who felt moved to inform Jimmy's wife that Jimmy was having an affair, one of the many. The man himself had been having an affair with the same woman for years--in fact, had a child with her--so Jimmy retaliated and told this man's wife as well as his own wife about that affair and the love child (my guess is that both wives probably knew all this already). Jimmy's outrage was about the adulterer calling Jimmy out for what Jimmy saw as his own lesser offense (brief dalliance, no child). My outrage when he told me the story was about the love child, a young teenage girl, suddenly having to confront this situation, talk of the town courtesy of Jimmy's wife, a story that was best kept secret for all concerned. Jimmy grudgingly acknowledged this but pointed out with some skewed logic that there would *be* no love child if this guy were honorable (define *honorable*).

There was sort of a theme to this story--Jimmy seeing the world as devious and immoral, ostensibly respectable people faulting him for behaviors of which they themselves were guilty--perhaps more guilty (if these behaviors were to be measured in degrees)--than Jimmy. They condemn me for doing what they do in secret was what he was saying. Their hypocrisy is no excuse for your immorality, I would reply. He didn't like that and would launch onto another rationalization when I said that. This was the "scholarship wife" theme that he used on occasion--that went thusly: His first wife, mother of his children, had been on a matrimonial scholarship. This was asserted with great scorn. While he worked and slaved on the floor of the New York Stock Exchange and scrambled for every penny, every billion pennies, I would add, his wife sat home by the pool with a maid, a nanny, a masseuse and an endless take-out menu. Well, I would say, you got to sit by that pool, too, play golf, take vacations, get chauffeur-driven to work and screw women when you felt like it. At least your so-called scholarship wife didn't screw other men. So, your logic is biased. We never concluded these discussions. We just dropped them. Neither of us took them personally, which was odd, considering the deep moral implications.

I sometimes thought about Jimmy's two previous marriages, how they contrasted, and where I fit on the scale. The first marriage was of the conventional design--church wedding, stay-at-home-wife and mother, working dad, three children and but for Jimmy's bizarre womanizing and reputation for behaving badly in general, would have been a classic example of what I have been calling the Father-Knows-Best model of the 1950s. The second marriage to Mary Lou resulted from his grand affair with her that ended the first marriage and approached the trophy-wife category--except for the fact that Jimmy's first wife had been a Vogue model and was very much trophy material herself. Jimmy obviously cared deeply for the lovely Mary Lou and never quite got over their split, a split he took credit for but that I was inclined to think was all Mary Lou's doing. Jimmy would narrate little post-divorce episodes, attempts at reconciliation ending in spitfire battles, and delighted in telling me of occasions on which he had seen Mary Lou while he and I first started dating. I asked once if he were telling me this out of kindness and he looked confused by the question.

I got the impression that Mary Lou, whom I never met, was every bit as volatile as Jimmy and fiercely dedicated to proving that she would not be dominated, cheated on, ignored, embarrassed--or any of the other things that Jimmy had seemed to take delight in doing to his first wife. Jimmy told me about a Super Bowl party he and Mary Lou had attended, a party she did not really wish to attend, where she sat in a corner reading a book while everyone else watched the game on various television screens throughout the house. Do you believe she did that, he asked me? Well--yes, I said, kind of obvious bratty get-back behavior. But asking why you would ever marry someone who didn't like the Super Bowl, I said, is more to the point. I held the romantic view for a while that Jimmy was so blinded by her beauty and his lust that he never paused to consider their almost total and absolute incompatibility. Then I decided that almost all men who divorced their first wives for younger blondes are similarly blinded and, most of all, I didn't really care. The lovely Mary Lou was gone, from what I could tell, and if she and Jimmy *were* having secret trysts--well, that was something else I never knew and eventually did not care about.

Where I fit into this wives' spectrum was not, and perhaps still isn't, clear to me. Christie used to tell me that of all her father's wives, I handled him best--sensibly and with stability. I considered this view. It was, from one perspective, horribly insulting, made me sound like the comfortable slippers prototype. But I understood what Christie meant. I wasn't afraid of Jimmy as his first wife had been (in the women-obey-your-husbands mode) and was not out to "tame" him as his second wife had been. I really had been looking for something authentic and, oddly, because we were well suited in a lot more ways than people would think

(I loved the Super Bowl, he made me laugh, we both hated Nixon, we liked to talk finance and politics, just for openers), I think we really did have a shot at authenticity. This was before I learned how emotionally damaged Jimmy really was--and, I guess, how I simply did not have the tolerance or the patience to work on remediating that damage--if, in fact, it could have been remediated. I know millions of women are married to damaged men (and vice versa) and live with it or manage it or work to change things--and that many of these spouses succeed in making good marriages, in whole or in part; so I take the blame for lacking whatever it took to stick it out. I do. This is not a story about blame, however; it's strictly a love story, in case you haven't figured that out yet.

So, in the end, I was just the third wife, unlike the first two maybe, but very like them in one singularly important way: I, too, was eventually an ex-wife.

CHAPTER 23

After Melissa died, I didn't hear from Jimmy for a long time, maybe for a year or so. I didn't hear much from Christie, either, but during one brief phone call she did mention that Jimmy had been spending a lot of time with Melissa's family since her death, especially with her son, and her brother and his wife, and that he had been helping dispose of her estate down in Florida--the house, cars, personal belongings and the like. So, Christie, I asked, there really was a Melissa, right? Oh yes, I think so Christie said and seemed a bit surprised at the question. But I never met her, she added. When I asked her how long Jimmy had been seeing Melissa before she died, Christie didn't actually know, but when we compared notes on things we did know, it seemed as if it might have been about six months or less. Not long for such devotion, I thought. Then I reminded myself that even this was bait and not to take it. Jimmy and the memory of him would always require this of me: vigilance. Getting an emotional charge of any kind from his bad or weird behavior was just another of his many hooks and to keep the friendship in tact, I had to keep things straight and avoid the barbed wire. He knew her; he loved her; she died. Just the facts, ma'am. It was a long time between our phone calls that year and increasingly longer between visits, so keeping things straight didn't require a lot of energy; just vigilance.

Time was passing. We had been divorced for about nine years by this time; I had my new house, my little dog, and a man in my life whom I saw fairly regularly. He was well-known to me, reliable, a good person, someone I would probably never marry but someone I knew could be in my life comfortably for a long time. I had recently made a career change, moving out of academics and into administration--same college, different environment entirely. The move suited me at my age and situation in life. I had also started looking for a vacation home, a get away place that would eliminate the need for the Florida rentals. Bella and I were actively looking in north Florida and in South Carolina and had made some nice trips to nice places in pursuit of our elusive vacation home. Over these years, I had developed feelings of settlement and contentment, not thinking this stasis was the worst thing that could ever happen to me-- but, in fact, thinking that it was something desirable and gratifying, that it felt a lot like peace.

My dear friend Eileen had died right about the time I was moving into my new house. Her death was a catastrophic event for me, mourned to this day. It was just one of those losses that leaves a hole in you that is never filled. Also, I had stopped seeing Dr. Waxman. It happened slowly. I missed an appointment and then had to cancel the make-up date and finally I just waited so long to make another appointment that I began to feel that I was OK, so I made a final appointment to be sure our separation was in order and it seems that it was. And I knew I could always go back.

And then, Jimmy got lung cancer. He called to tell me about it and seemed strangely detached. He was not going to have surgery--just radiation and chemo. I thought that sounded like good news but then discovered why and it turned out to be not such good news. Quite the reverse: His tumors were inoperable. He did very well for a long time, two years at least, stayed well, busy and active, and stayed in touch, and we talked often. He was very happy about Bella's engagement when I called to tell him about it and although he lived for more than a year after her wedding, was too unwell by the time of the ceremony to make the trip from Florida to Connecticut, where Bella and Mark were married. It was a lovely wedding and in the midst of it, I stopped and thought how Bella's father, my cherished first husband, would have loved it--and then, as a small afterthought, that Jimmy would have loved it, too.

Eventually, I heard from Christie who was in Florida and had called to tell me that her Dad was not doing well at all and although he lingered on in a nursing facility for some months, it was clear he was not going to get better. I asked Christie if I should come down and she said she didn't really need any assistance and it was never mentioned that Jimmy had asked for me or mentioned me at all. He probably hadn't. At any rate, I didn't go, he died, and I regretted not going forever. The going would have been more for me than for him, and he may not even have known me by that time. But we don't always get things right.

And that was always there underneath our story, wasn't it--both of us getting a great deal wrong, seldom caring in the right way or perhaps not knowing how? And in the end, regardless of all the pain and the craziness, regardless of all the fear and all the frustration that he introduced into my mid-life, the loss of him also left a hole in me that will never be filled. It just worked out that way. I don't know why. I will never know whether he was a great love or a great waste of my time--whether he was both or he was neither. Because that's the way life always is.

Printed in the United States
By Bookmasters